What's a Lady Got to Do to Fulfill Her Life?

by

Felicity Talisman

Passport to Pleasure Series

Dedication

To Bruce, for his enthusiastic support.

To Jean, for her wonderful review and after all she's gone through, still smiles and gets on with it enjoying life to the fullest. To all those out there that when life served up an unexpected curveball, had the guts to pick up the pieces and get on with it.

To Jenny, for standing by, doing the editing and believing in me and my craziness.

Prelude

"Leanne Benson?"

"Yes."

"I'm Dr. Johnson from Cedars-Sinai Hospital. I hate to inform you that we were called to your father's house, Robert Benson, late last night by the alarm company." The man's tone was devoid of warmth.

"Was he broken into? Is he okay?" Leanne gasped as she was getting ready to head out the door for work. A glance at the wall clock told her she wasn't late yet.

"No, apparently Robert set off the house alarm, calling the alarm company that he was having a heart attack." The displaced voice on the other end of the phone line continued with that emotionless voice.

"What do you mean having, is he okay?" Her dad hadn't been getting along well, health-wise since her mom passed away last year. Leanne and her husband Ben had been trying to get him into a nursing home, although he looked well the last time she visited. He was too stubborn to leave and how could she blame him, all of his children had grown up in that house.

Speaking of Ben, where was he? Wasn't he supposed to be home by now from his business flight out of New York? Maybe it was delayed—she'd call in a minute.

"I'm afraid he died before we could get him to the hospital." Cold and distant. How many times had he called with news as tragic as this to other people?

"Wha…" Leanne stared stunned at her cell phone as it beeped, alerting her via her house monitor app that someone was at her front door.

The front doorbell rang a second later. "Crap, better not be some bloody salesman at this time of the day. At least not now, anyway."

One always expects the worst when their parents get old, but expecting and experiencing it is quite different. Tears threatened as realizations kicked in. Robert, her dad, the man that had always been there for her, was gone.

Numbness ran through her as she pulled up the camera image on her app. It was the police. No doubt to let her know about her dad.

"Ah, gotta go. The police are here at the door, probably to tell me the same news you just did. I'll call back in a second." She clicked off her phone before a response could be made and strolled to the front door, fighting back the tears. Leanne opened the door and stared into the face of a handsome, square-jawed officer.

"Hi, Mrs. Benson, I'm here to inform you…"

"Yeah, I just heard. My father passed away."

The handsome cop looked at her quizzically and down at the paper he held. "Ah, yes, ma'am, news can travel fast these days. He suffered massive internal injuries, and there was nothing the hospital could do. I'm so sorry."

"Massive internal injuries, from a heart attack?"

"Heart attack? No, from the car crash he was in."

"What? He was at home. I just got a call from the hospital."

The police officer winced, glanced at her oddly, and looked at the paper in his hands. "Does your father drive a Mercedes AMG Roadster License plate 3247 HWV?"

"Ah, no, that's my husband's car." Her heart thumped hard.

"Is your husband, Ben Benson?"

"Yes." As she looked ahead, everything started swirling in a dizzying motion.

"I'm so sorry to inform you that Ben Benson died from injuries sustained in a vehicular accident at six-ten this morning."

Her legs wobbled, and the world spun away. The officer struggled to catch Leanne as she slumped to the ground.

Chapter One

Tears streamed down Leanne's face as she walked through her dad's house. It had been a month since he'd passed away. Her brother and sister had agreed to sell the place and split the money. The will specifically stated all three were to receive his estate evenly. She didn't really care. It wouldn't bring him or her mother, who'd passed away last year, back.

Nor would it bring back Ben. She could barely come to terms with one, let alone the other. Especially at a time when she could really use Ben's shoulder to lean or cry on.

Her sister Kathy walked up to Leanne as she stared at the prints her mom loved on the wall of their house. Set in the 1920s, they were from another era of art déco. Everyone seemed happy, money flowed freely, fashions, and being fashionable decorated the magazines. Some were from tourist destinations of the time, including the mountain resorts, railroad destinations, and two places where Leanne always wanted to go, but hadn't—Lake Louise and Banff Springs Hotel in the Canadian Rockies. Everything seemed simpler and easier before the big crash and the starving thirties that followed. Definitely another era of a time even before her parents met.

Life, until last year, had been quite the struggle. The American recession had hit her business, house selling and buying, very hard even in the land of the rich and extravagant Hollywood. Leanne, after being approached by a customer, had come up with the idea to offer special services to her ultra-rich clients, and she'd sold many places in the last year.

Ben and she were getting along better than ever. He was the type of guy who got excited knowing his wife was having sex with another man, or even better, another woman. After one of his long business trips, she'd regale him with one of her customer's exploits, which usually ended with him getting very aroused and a passionate night of hot lovemaking. As for herself, Leanne enjoyed what she called, cheating with hubby's approval, especially after her first couple of encounters with another female. She'd sometimes fantasized about it but had never acted on it, much to Ben's chagrin, until she was seduced by Sam, a gorgeous woman who ran a lingerie store. Leanne had on occasion told Ben bedtime stories of her and someone else before they made love, many times in the past.

Had, but not anymore.

They'd even begun to think of kids. Just when everything seemed to be coming around and beginning to smell like roses, her life was thrown completely upside down.

Now, after the payout on Ben's insurance policies and her dad's estate, she had more than enough money to do any crazy bucket-list thing or holiday she ever wanted. Only there was no one to share it with and 'nothing seemed to matter right about now. She stared at the inexpensive prints of her mom, Irene's. Leanne knew she loved those, and no matter how many times they moved or redecorated, she would never part with them. Did she have anything in her life that mattered that much? Tears streamed down her face. That was the problem. She didn't have anything she really wanted to do with herself.

"You okay? Can't imagine what you're going through with burying Ben two weeks ago and now this. I'm having a hard time coping with just knowing Dad and Mom are gone. Leanne?" her sister, Deborah, asked.

She simply stared at the prints as her mother's words from her diaries whispered in her ears. She'd read them all this week. One of the things that her mom wanted Leanne to have after they both passed away was the dairies of her travels. Irene had always written her travels and holidays in a journal. Her thoughts, feelings, commenting that ordinary life wasn't worth mentioning. To her surprise, she discovered her mom had a hidden talent for both writing and drawing, as she flipped through the pages of her journals. Obviously, it was where Leanne got her artistic skills from. She knew her mom always regretted not pursuing either her writing or drawings. Back then, women weren't encouraged to do more than look after the family and their man.

Leanne pursed her lips. She'd done the same, too busy with her career to put time aside to pursue the drawing that she loved to do but rarely did. *Was I any different from Mom in that respect?* In Mom's day, it was a different culture—the woman stayed at home and raised the kids. Leanne sighed, in the age of liberation, *was I any better?* At least she had the choice to do more with her life. *Mom never did.*

She and Ben were talking about starting a family

this year. Her career and business had taken off. He'd been doing quite well as a bank manager.

Now, all gone.

Ben was big on insurance and had several policies stored in their safety deposit box. She gave those all to her lawyer to deal with.

Her dad's estate was worth millions. Still, what did it matter? The money and security that she fought so hard to earn all her life she now had. Leanne stared at the prints. Only everyone around her was gone. Tears streamed down her face as she downed her glass of wine in one long guzzle. None of this material stuff really mattered, did it? When there was no one to share it with. It was just stuff.

Tears unleashed down her face. She couldn't take it anymore and had to get out, away from here. "You guys decide what you want. All I want are these two prints. Put the sale of the estate into my account, and whatever you don't want, just donate to the Goodwill store."

Her sister stood stunned as Leanne grabbed the two framed prints off the wall and stormed out. She couldn't take being in the house anymore. The memories of two loving parents, growing up in this house, her entire childhood not gone, but at an end. Her first kiss with Ben. Here in this house. Gone. The moment she knew he was the one. Gone. All gone into the vaults of her memories.

So lost, I feel so lost and empty.

Leanne placed the prints on the front passenger seat of her BMW and sobbed uncontrollably. Everything cut away, except work. She dabbed a tissue on her cheeks, trying to look civil. For the most part, she'd held herself together when out in public, until today. She didn't realize being in that house would be so hard.

That house.

What a thing to say.

Should be, was, her life until now.

All gone.

What had possessed her to storm out with a pair of lousy twenty-dollar prints? She stared at the scene from Lake Louise, painted in art deco shades of brown, purples, and blues. One woman in full dress on the window ledge and another in riding gear, perhaps just getting ready to ride a horse around the lake or in some lewd story she'd relate to Ben, something kinkier. Both intent on the view of Mt. Victoria at the rear of Lake Louise. Her mother's words from her diary. A diary that she never knew she kept, that Leanne read just in the last few days.

I stare today out the window of the Prince of Wales Hotel at the serene beauty of Lake Louise. Named after Princess Louise Caroline Alberta. Words do little to express the serenity here. Mountains fall away straight into the pastel blue of the lake, as if unable to stop itself, needing to wash its base in the clear waters. If this was in England, The Lady Of The Lake, Evienne or Viviane, as she is usually called, would come walking gracefully out of the waters, sword held high to give to Arthur. Men would bow to her beauty and swear allegiance to her.

Mt. Victoria, at the rear of the lake, stands as a restless former lover, waiting his turn again to kiss the feet of Louise's waters. They say if you stand outside as the sun sets behind the hotel, you can hear music playing in the air. I've heard it, soft hums and sweet voices, like angels singing in peace. Nothing quite as serene, when everything is still and the earth is singing its joy to you.

July 5th, 1948

All Leanne knew was she'd never experienced anything quite like that. She was going to go there, stare out the same window as her mother did and this woman, gazing in wonder at the beauty of Lake Louise. She'd sit on those shores someday and paint what her mom saw and felt.

Yes, work was the only thing that had begun to go positive this year and something she could throw herself into and get lost in. She had to thank Sam for that, and perhaps she could be more than a shoulder to cry on. Leanne clicked on her seatbelt and drove straight to 'A Lady's Nice Things' lingerie store.

****

Sam took one look at Leanne as she walked in, holding the two prints from her parents' home in her hands. Streaks of mascara stained her cheeks. "God, honey, you've had a rough day, haven't you?"

Leanne didn't have to look in the mirror to know she looked like a rag doll pulled out of a junkyard.

"Jasmine, we're not to be disturbed. If we're not out before closing, lock up," Sam told her employee, a young, vivacious blonde. She pulled Leanne into the back of the store.

Sam closed the door to the backroom. "Lady, you need one helluva stiff drink." She knew what had happened through Janice, her partner and lover, who also worked with Leanne when she needed it, which was a lot in the last month.

Leanne put the two prints down, tumbling onto the

9

sofa she and Sam had made love on last year when Sam had seduced her. Her first lesbian experience and one that completely changed her views on her own sexuality.

Leanne sat there as she grabbed a tissue and tried to dry away tears, which only streaked her makeup even more. She drank deep from the wineglass and sat stunned, staring at the pictures as Sam sat beside her. "I feel so lost, so cut from everything I once knew."

Sam patted her leg. "Well, you're in pain and that's okay. It's the first part of healing. Let it out, lady." She reached up and stroked Leanne's hair.

Tears continued to stream down the redhead's face. "Dad, I half expected. Ben was such a total shock."

"I know." Sam let Leanne babble incoherently for several minutes. She told her about her mom's diary, taking the prints and storming out.

Finally done, Leanne sobbed in silence as Sam got up to get her another glass of wine.

"Tell me about those pictures you've got?" she asked as she sat down.

Leanne sipped deeply of the dry Merlot. "My mom's, the only thing I wanted from the house. Don't know what it is, the serenity, something I haven't got right now. I've always been good at drawing and thought when I get older I'd like to paint pictures similar to these. My mom had an artistic desire she never fulfilled. I didn't know.

"I recently read 'her diaries, which I never knew she kept, and I doubt Dad did either. She talked about this place when she was very young. Mom went on a holiday up the Canadian Rockies and ended up meeting Dad there. That lady in the painting seems so at peace staring out that window I could picture Mom staring out the window. I never really looked at these pictures, nor knew their meaning until they both passed away. I don't ever remember Irene telling me the history of these pictures. Another age, another time, different from my parents."

"So it can be another time, another age for you."

"What are you saying, Sam?"

"I'm going to assume your hubby had insurance coverage." "Yes, and Dad was well off."

"The real estate business you could bury yourself into, and probably already have, which I'd expect. But Janice could look after the place, run it for you, for a couple of months. You have no reason to stay here—you've unlimited resources. You did say you like to draw."

Leanne nodded blankly, the wineglass warming in her hand as she stared into its ruby depths.

"You need focus, something to put direction into your life. That picture is your mom's way of telling you, no kicking your ass into getting a shift on."

"Think so?"

"Lady, I can see it, and I don't have blonde roots."

Leanne thought about the picture. Her mom's musings of being there in her journals.

"If nothing else, go there. See Lake Louise for yourself. I think I've heard something about a school of fine arts in the area around Banff. Probably some of the best teachers in the world. Pack your bags and go find yourself. Something awaits you there, I know it. Your mom's way of telling you not to be like her.

"You're a smart lady and from what you told me, your mother wasted her talents. Well, this is the twenty-

11

first century and things have changed. So don't make her mistakes all over again. Do what your heart and your mother know it must!"

Leanne frowned. "You're right. I'm going to check out their courses and drive there. Could use the alone time in the car. It would give me time to think and sort out my feelings. Ben and I had driven along the California coast a few times. We talked about doing a road trip, just thought it would be together." She pursed her lips as tears threatened to flood down her face again.

"Hey, none of that. This is Samantha's two-step program to getting on with your life."

"Okay, I'm buying it, and I've got the great cruising car for it. My Beamer. I can already see myself top down, music blaring away. What do you mean two-step?" Leanne turned to look at the buxom woman.

Sam leaned over and kissed her softly on the lips as she caressed Leanne's arm. "Now that's the Leanne I know. Step one is getting rid of some of that stress you've built up over the last month or so." She turned Leanne's face to herself and kissed her, slow and sensual. "I'll bet with all this crap going down you haven't had any pleasure, have you?"

Leanne's cheeks flushed. She hadn't been kissed in the last few weeks and the batteries were definitely rusting away in Big Jimmy, her vibrator. The heat in Sam's lips sent erotic shivers down her belly. "No, and to be honest, haven't felt like it. The suffering kinda gets in the way of feeling sexy."

"So step one is me getting you to release those built-up stresses and buried desires behind those attention-starved lips. Give me a few minutes and I'll have you on the recovery band wagon to feeling horny and desired again. I'll let Jasmine know I'll be here late with you, and be right back."

Leanne stared at her mom's prints. Could she do it? Drive to another country, by herself? Leanne smiled as Sam walked back into the room. She had to for herself and her mom's sake. Leanne asked as Sam locked the door behind her. "Jasmine is a gorgeous young lady, have you?"

"Well, let's just say she is rather yummy and in order to better serve my customers, some in more, ah, intimate matters of undergarments, she has to enjoy the female figure. Some of my richer customers expect, like you do, a more personal touch, not to mention they tip rather well. I've lost more than one assistant over the years to customers who insisted on having, shall we say, better in house service."

Leanne squinted at Sam, not quite understanding.

"Let's say some well-to-do women pay very well to have a gorgeous young lady to clean their house and service their needs."

"Good God, she looks like she could be a cheerleader. Doesn't Janice get upset?"

"Have I gotten jealous about some of the stuff you and Janice have gotten into?" Sam questioned.

Leanne thought about the role-play with an actress once and how they tied her up, seduced her against her will, dominated her, and made love after in the rental van. Leanne being ridden by Janice and her large strap-on. She knew Janice told Sam everything. "Point well taken. Maybe that's what I need, someone that doesn't get jealous and is open to me having other partners or at least delicious women like you in my life. Now, what was it you were going to do to ease my strife?" Until Sam's kiss, she hadn't realized how keyed up she'd become in the last few weeks.

"Oh, I see I've piqued your interest." Sam moved to the small stereo and put on some relaxing, sensual music, reminding Leanne of Enya. The smell of incense filtered into the air as she lit a cone and slowly spread a blanket on the floor. Refilling her wine, Sam pulled a couple of vials of oils from her drawer and placed them on the blanket. She reached back and undid her dress, letting it fall to the floor. "Don't want this expensive dress to get oil all over it, do I?" She stood there in a violet G-string and bra that did little to conceal her massive cleavage.

Leanne watched, mesmerized, 'having forgotten how gorgeous a body Sam had. She worked out often and it showed. Her well-toned, darkly tanned body reflected off the candles she lit one at a time and finally turned off the lights.

"Now, lady, on the blanket, naked," she said, more a command than a request. Leanne felt a stir inside—she remembered the night at Sam and Janice's place where Sam was the dominatrix, her and Janice the subservient one's who had to perform as requested in order to satisfy Sam's needs. A deep erotic thrill stirred some part of her at being dominated by this or other strong women. "I'm going to begin by giving you a massage."

Leanne rose and stripped herself naked. She wasn't self-conscious about Sam looking at her, not after all the times they'd made love. She lay down on her stomach, hands by her side. The music and incense worked their way into her grief-stricken nerves, relaxing her more than anything she'd felt in the last month. How much stress had she been carrying without realizing it? The pain of recent events ebbed away as she inhaled the sandalwood and patchouli incense.

Sam's strong hands kneaded the fragrant oils into her shoulders. Leanne surrendered to Sam's massage, her anxieties washing away. The wine mellowed her, stole her away on the soft tones rolling through the room. Leanne slipped into a semi-conscious state as Sam's fingers worked their way down her arms, back, and thighs, finding every tight muscle in her body and working out all the knots life had thrown at her lately. "If you haven't guessed, I used to do massages in my younger days."

A grunt of pleasure was all she could manage as she drifted further into a dreamlike state. Her body aches and pains kneaded away on the cadence of soft music and sandalwood breezes.

Warm breath on the sole of her left foot brought Leanne back from her world of daydreams as she felt Sam's tongue across the arch of her foot. Her mouth closed over Leanne's small toe and sucked softly. "Oh," escaped from her lips. *It has been way too long since I've had an orgasm.*

Arousal throbbed through her, bringing its hungry appetite that hadn't been addressed in such a long time. Leanne groaned as Sam continued licking and sucking at her toes gently. Long moments of wet tongue and soft lips sucking away at intimate places she never knew could be that exciting to caress. Leanne moaned loudly, as her wetness built quickly. This was one of the most erotic experiences she'd ever had.

"I take it you like that?"

"Oh, yes. Is this part of your massage?"

"Just for my more intimate partners."

Leanne gasped again as Sam's lips surrounded her big toe and slowly slid down, like it was an erect cock.

"Lucky Janice."

Sam was right—she hadn't been touched sexually by herself or anyone in weeks, nor had she felt the urge until now. Sam's tongue and fingers played across her toes and feet, licking and sucking slowly as if Leanne had a cock and she was performing fellatio to get her off. Cravings she hadn't had in so long flared to life, dark urges needing satiating. It had been far too long.

Sam spread her legs apart and rubbed the inside of her calves and thighs, this time softer, more caressing than kneading. Working her way up her body toward the center of Leanne's building hungers. Oiled hands rubbed her rear, worked toward her anus, and rubbed the dark crease between before sliding down to the wetness throbbing at Leanne's slit. She began to finger her clit slowly. Leanne could feel herself beginning to build as Sam moved a hand back to her anus and slipped an oiled finger inside.

"Oh," Leanne groaned, giving herself totally to the woman masturbating her in both orifices. The sheer eroticism so long denied, sexual hungers not allowed, nor barely remembered in what seemed like such a long time, thundered to life with great demanding need. Spreading her legs more and feeling the orgasm erupting inside, Leanne humped against Sam's hands, surrendering. She shuddered as her orgasm erupted quickly, unexpectedly with thunderstorm intensity. Sam kept at it as Leanne convulsed, lost in the throes of one of the most powerful orgasms she ever had.

As it subsided, Sam leaned over her large breasts, gliding against Leanne's back as she planted soft kisses on her ear, her lips, their bodies melding together in a comforting embrace. As Sam rubbed between them, the oils caused a warm sensation to spread across their skins.

"Can I return the favor?" She wanted to be between her legs, licking Sam's swollen pussy.

"No, tonight is about you. Now get up on all fours."

Leanne did, and Sam kissed each of her cheeks, tongue licked away first around the brown whirl of her anus, then lower along the wet slit of her pussy lips. She alternated between licking her, sucking on the awoken lips of her labia and sucking delicately on her clit. Slower this time, Leanne could feel herself build again as a softer orgasm went through her, leaving her in a shuddering state cresting over and over like the ocean beaching itself on rocky cliffs. Finally, she cried, "Stop." Leanne collapsed to her stomach, overwhelmed by the trembling pleasures rippling through her. Tears unexpectedly ran down her cheeks.

Sam moved beside her and just hugged her as she kissed her forehead and wiped away the salty tears.

"Oh God, I didn't realize how much I needed that," Leanne finally spoke, kissing her friend as Sam held her.

"Ah, what are friends for?" Sam smiled and held her, the sensual fragrances of the incense wafting through the air.

"You sure you don't want me to return the favor?"

"No, I'll take it out on Janice when I get home."

"Lucky girl."

Leanne smiled. "Thanks." She kissed Sam tenderly on the mouth. "I'll talk to Janice at the office tomorrow about looking after the business while I take some time off."

"That's the woman I know. Now, time to get dressed, put your big girl pants on, and figure out what it is you need to discover about yourself, and what you want to do with your life. I always say expect the unexpected and who knows, maybe you'll find a handsome park ranger in the wild Canadian Rockies."

"God, after tonight maybe a Rangeress." Or Lady of the Lake, she thought, with or without her sword to impale her.

Getting home, she packed up what she thought she needed, making sure she also grabbed her passport if needed. "Tomorrow brings a whole new adventure."

Chapter Two

Leanne had spent the last two days driving up the Northern California coast, visiting a couple of wineries, and hiking the Redwoods. To be told they were the biggest trees in the world, but to be standing at the base of one of these towering giants, looking up and not being able to spot the tops was another thing. Like the giant beanstalks in the fairy tale, they just went up into the air forever. Knowing these trees have been here for over a thousand years, as she walked around the massive craggy base, made her life and herself seem miniscule.

Leanne even rented a quad and spent a half day bombing up and down the sand dunes south of Florence, in southern Oregon. She had listened to the raucous bellow of Sea Lions in the caves and stared at many a windswept beach behind the wheel of her BMW. Seagulls squawked, waves sighed away, and sunshine washed over her. All the places Ben never cared for, she finally visited on her own. Why was that?

The places she always wanted to see. Did he, their finances, or herself, stop her? She knew that if he couldn't have come along, he'd have gladly encouraged her to do it on her own.

That was the sad part, Leanne thought as she checked into the Nye Beach Hotel at Nye Beach in Newport, Oregon. The only one that had stopped her was herself. She hadn't the guts or the inclination to do things she always wanted to and like her mother, had let everything else rule her desires.

An artist's retreat, one of her friends, who had told her about this place, called it. She glanced at a cat curled on a chair warming in the sun at the foot of an old set of wooden stairs, that she already knew creaked when you stepped on them.

"That's Shelley, and she's not a mouser," the innkeeper stated, "she's a sun-catcher cat. Wherever the sun is, she catches it."

She'd spent the last couple of nights in nondescript nationally branded motels, where you knew the bars of soap and the plastic coffee makers were all the same.

"Much unlike the author." Leanne breathed deeply, the smell of age, of musty volumes, and something vaguely familiar about the place hung in the air. Like she'd walked into it in another lifetime. The building she knew was over a hundred years old, built somewhere in the time of Lake Louise, the Banff hotels, and the prints she had stashed in the backseat. "My friend Maureen came here years ago and she was overwhelmed by it. She bragged about how relaxing it was here, a real artist's retreat, to rebuild your muse, inspire creativity, or just flake out and relax. But she suggested, be careful, this place either comforts you or spits you out."

"Your friend is right. You either love it or hate it here." The older lady smiled at her. She'd already been sucked in.

"Do you have Wi-Fi?"

"Pfftt. We don't have internet, phones or even TV. Instead, at night, the sound of old bards' footsteps creak in the hall reciting their next novel, and you fall asleep to the lullaby of the ocean crashing to the beach. Upstairs, 'there are games and puzzles to play, along with coffee, tea, and mulled wine in the library after ten p.m. Will that do?"

Leanne had forgotten what her friend had said about the mulled hot wine served at night. She can already taste the sweet tinge of cinnamon and heady musk of cloves going down her throat. "Well, as long as I don't have to drink Dickens under the table, this is my idea of perfect."

"I warn you Dickens isn't the worry." The Innkeeper leaned closer. "I'd stay away from playing cards with Dr. Seuss. He keeps changing the rules to three eggs and ham and even if you win you don't want to have to eat anything green." She laughed, grabbed Leanne's bags, and headed for her room, the Claudine.

They passed Jules Verne's room as the ocean crashed in the background, hopefully not from his room, and winked at Mrs. Jo Rowling as sparks fluttered from wand to wand in hers, The Gryffindor, which should really be the name of a hotel not a room in an inn, Leanne thought. Character, that's what it was, original character, and indeed she was pulled in.

Every one of the twenty-some rooms she knew was dedicated to an author or a novel. Ben had no designs on ever coming here, yet something about it, being surrounded by all these artists, called to her, and with him gone, sadness tugged. She wanted to begin her drawings here, up in the library or on the beach for the next few nights.

Throwing her luggage on to the bed, she wanted to explore the hotel and the area before settling down. The ocean crashed in the background as she walked out onto the balcony. White surf-like stallions' manes streaming in the wind, raced forward to end their brief lifespan thundering into the beach. She missed Ben, they'd driven the Big Sur coast a couple of times when they first met, just the two of them, alone on beaches as surf cascaded to shore. Making love on the sand, she winced, sometimes a little painful—it was amazing how sand got in hidden crevices. In the last few years, they hadn't done anything spontaneous like that. Well, at least until Leanne made love to Ben in a client's bedroom, while the woman watched on the balcony getting herself off. Leanne sighed, tears threatened as she worked her way up to the library on the third floor.

The last few months were the best they had together. What started as a crazy idea of selling something extra as part of the property, usually weird sexy escapades that only happened in Hollywood, not only took off but also brought some needed heat back into their own sex life. Boy, did she quickly find out what that kinky side of town was like and what people were willing to pay. More than getting her and Ben closer to each other, it generated a lot of sales as well.

The hardest part of him being gone was her rolling over in the dark and feeling only the lonely, cold bed at night.

Leanne gasped at the opulence of her private-balconied room. Wrap-around ornate picture windows provided a stunning view of the beach and the ocean beyond. She envisioned herself reclining on the bed, a glass of ice-cold Chardonnay in hand, viewing whales spouting and lovers hugging each other. Leanne smiled jealously. Maybe that would be her someday again soon, but not this day. This day was about finding the uniqueness that was her inside. Her next stop would be going further up the coast, visiting Oregon's famous Cannon Beach before going into Canada and seeing famous Vancouver for the first time.

She wandered about the room, flipping through some of the writer's books. They had, among Collette's many books she wrote in her lifetime, the Claudine series of four books. Written about a woman who grew from a child to finding herself, to her awakening sexuality, to her husband, to the arms of a dominating woman. "Oh, that could be a good read for later." She smiled, after some of her escapades with women she wondered if men were worth the trouble. She'd read about Collette, back in the turn of the last century, she'd scandalized Paris by kissing a girl on stage, and while the writer had been married a couple of times, she'd been known to have several lesbian affairs.

Sounds like my kind of woman. This may have to do. It's about as close to a lover as I'll get tonight. She frowned and stared at the bed. Sadness welled up inside. It wasn't easy to be positive when all that's inside are memories cut short. What hurt the most was the fact that she never even had the chance to say goodbye or 'I love you' to Ben.

Okay, enough of the pity—time to check out the rest of the hotel.

After unpacking, Leanne walked around the hotel gift area. Chatting with the front desk, she discovered that they had special set dinner meals every night in the dining room. Leanne went upstairs to the third-floor library where little ceramic suns dangled. There were other rooms as well, of unfinished puzzles, sofas and a fireplace. Outside seagulls squawked in mock soliloquy, as she poured herself a cup of the heady robust coffee from the urns set out in one of the puzzle rooms. Ben used to like his coffee, strong, like this. Used to.

I've got to quit feeling sorry for myself. The only person I'm going to attract is Eeyore, with this sad face. Leanne fought back tears as an older man, oddly dressed in a dark green suit jacket, khaki pants, and red woolly socks, stared out the window and caught her attention. "Sorry, I didn't mean to disturb you." How long, she wondered, before the memory of Ben faded and just she remained? Her eyes, she knew were puffy with redness, Leanne tried not to radiate her misery outward but surely he was bound to notice.

"I was just wondering if the seagulls were squawking at me. However, I see most likely it was you instead." He bluntly and a bit rudely said to her.

Older, late forties, handsome. One of those men who probably looked boyish or gangly when young, yet filled out with age, some gray at the temples, accented a certain classiness. Not unlike someone such as Jon Bon Jovi as he is now, as opposed to when he was younger.

Life seemed cruel to the sexes. It made many men more handsome, distinguished, while many women became gray-haired, saggy-breasted, and a few pounds heavier from their childbearing years. *I dread getting older. Thank God for peroxide and plastic surgery.* "At me. Why would you say such a thing?" She frowned, suddenly put off.

"Got your mind off the pain, didn't it."

Leanne quelled her rising anger. This was supposed to be a holiday, not a place to start something.

Besides, she had enough pain to deal with right now and didn't want to add to the misery. Still, he, in his own rude way, was obviously concerned.

"Oh, I like the fire behind those eyes. Most men think that translates to a woman full of lust. There's nothing quite like a lusty woman, ask Shakespeare or Yeats or a lusty female like Mae West."

Bastard, she thought under her breath, snapping, "Can't you see I'm here in pain? Grieving?"

"Can't you see I'm here laughing and enjoying my holiday? Good day, Lady Whatever-the-name-of-your-royal-highness-is? Oh, and there's nothing wrong with lust. A certain amount is good—makes you want to possess life from death. It drives you to not want to give up. Like cream brings the ones suited to succeed to the top. It tests, yeah."

Fucker. He'd hit her right between the eyes. Every business-orientated nerve told her to either shut up or let him talk or just simply say thanks and walk away. "Leanne!" she blurted out. He'd stirred something inside all right. *Even when the customer is an ass, he's always right.* Only she wasn't working and he was wrecking her vision of a holiday. *Damn the frigging customer.*

"What?"

"I'm Leanne Benson. I hate being called lady. My parents used to always say that when they were mad at me." She sniffled, wanting to add, *and now they're both gone, along with her husband.*

"Whew, thank God. For a second I thought you were going to say something like Austen or Eyre. Thinking I'm seeing ghosts and might actually be talking to one is another wholly different thing."

Leanne smiled slightly, a little massaged by his strange sense of humor. Wondering why the universe dragged this odd, slightly exasperating, and strangely-dressed man into her life?

"Ah, so you've lost someone then. Your parents?"

Leanne nodded and sipped at the deep, earthy aroma of her coffee. "Yes, and more. Isn't that why people cry? When they're in pain, dealing with a tragic loss in their lives."

"No, sometimes they cry over a good movie, their pets dying. Some cry over the best chocolate cake they ever ate. I knew a lady, err, woman, sorry, that cried with every orgasm she ever had."

"What? You're rude." Forget about the distinguished older look, perhaps he was just some handsome, uncouth rogue or scoundrel from many of the novels on the shelves behind them.

"No, I'm Tom. Rude was my brother George. I grew to truly appreciate downright belligerence from him. He could say things that would make priests blush and nuns wet their habits."

Leanne blinked, caught off guard, her mouth agape like someone loudly interrupted turning pages in a library book, not knowing what to say. "I, er, I…are you here by yourself or is there someone with you?"

"Well if you call a suitcase, dozens of seagulls, two people on the beach both badly overweight, thin on financial resources, and long on lovemaking, a porter who doesn't give a rat's ass about his job and only wants to catch the next Seattle Mariners' game being alone, then I'm alone. Oh, the cat. I forgot about the cat. He chases mice on crutches." Tom tapped his lip trying to look wisely pondering.

"He what?" The tears dried away as Leanne ground the tissue in her fingers and a smile threatened to break. He was either very observant or just nuts.

"Old friend once said, I've learned to chase fast whiskey and slow women in my maturity. So you call me alone if you like, no one is ever truly alone, depending on your perception of life. I think it's a big beautiful world out there. Wait. I think I did forget something." He patted his pockets. "Left it somewhere—now what was that?"

Leanne frowned as she watched him. "Left what?" Watching his hands, expecting a cheap magic trick. At this point, she figured he was capable of anything. *Yup, truly mad.*

"Ah, crap! My wife. I must have left her back in the pub." He laughed.

Leanne smiled weakly, Ben was a fan of Irish and English style pubs and while she hadn't visited the one up the street, that was next on her to-do list before leaving. Sadness welled inside, again. She wiped aside her tears on the well-worn tissue. She would have liked to have gone there with Ben.

"Sorry, it's like being in hell right now."

"Hell passes."

"Feels like forever." He'd stirred up a lot of what she attempted to keep buried inside. Perhaps it was just better to return to her room. At the moment, the pain threatened to make her a lot less than civil and she didn't want to be sobbing all over some complete stranger.

"Yeah, I'll bet they said that at the Alamo."

"What? You're a weird, off-putting man." She rudely stuffs the tissue in her pocket like a heavyweight boxer denied his knockout punch. He irritated her so much she wanted to slug him right between the pompous grin on his face and that devilishly handsome smile. *If he is trying to get me mad and off my pity party post, it's working.*

"Better than a sad excuse for a happy full-of-life woman." He beamed ear to ear.

"I think this conversation has ended." Leanne stormed by as her venom spate trails of hellfire behind her. Hands clenched, she was ready to claw his smug face.

"I think it has just begun. See you tonight. Mulled wine, fireplace, and me. Couldn't get any better."

"Not in a million years." She harrumphed in disgust as she headed down the stairs to her room. Still, he engaged her, she thought as she stormed down the stairs toward her room. He made her laugh and stirred her heart and her fire. It was more than anyone had done in a long time.

Leanne paced back and forth in her room, letting her anger subside. Grabbing her sketchpad and camera, she decided to go to the beach. She took several pictures of the hotel as she walked past, thinking she might want to paint or draw the building on this holiday. The pale yellow and green-blue outside reminded her of the Canadian Pacific Railway paintings she'd brought with her in the car for inspiration and condolence. Another time and place, back when times were simpler and easier—the roaring twenties.

She took a picture of the front and stared over her camera. There, in the Sherlock Holmes room, which was just under hers, a couple, both naked. The man thrust into her as the ocean crashed outside. Leanne ducked and scuttled down to the beach. Embarrassed, yet hoping that could be her. Other than Sam comforting her the other night, she hadn't any sexual thoughts or desires. Instead, she allowed too much grief to get in the way.

She propped herself against an old log and began to draw a picture of a couple, as she watched them making love at their window.

Lustful gazes lost in a sea of their internal passions, while the ocean crashed outside in white sheets of silk cascading to the shore ending in frothy carnations kissing each other. She penciled her vision in her mind's eye.

That was the thought that she wanted to paint. She could only wish that was her someday again, making love with her significant other.

Her rough draft looked more like two Eskimos lost in a snowstorm. Leanne smiled and packed up her paints. "Time to check out the town, get a pint at the Irish pub, and hopefully not meet Tom's wife before dinner." Because if she was as rude as him, she wouldn't hesitate taking an eye or two out.

****

It was late. Leanne stared out the third-story window. The sun had recently set, listening to the dull thunder of surf angels crashing to the beach as the sky darkened. The ocean's coldness licked at her through the single-paned glass as the cinnamon-infused spice of the wine tickled her nose, addling her mind and warming her belly. She spent the rest of the day wandering around town, visiting the little shops, bought a few objects for home, and had them shipped back. For dinner, she went for bangers and mash at Nana's the

Irish pub. It was Ben's favorite meal, her way of perhaps honoring his memory. God, she missed him. Watching couples laughing together, some it was obvious were on first dates. It only made the pain hurt worse. That and the internal sadness that seemed to haunt her. When would it leave? The only good thing was she hadn't spotted Tom anywhere in town and so far not here either. And yes, before he showed up, she knew he was behind her.

"Ah, I see you found the mulled wine they brew every night. Lolls the guests, staff and ghosts to sleep." Tom interrupted her musings. True to his word, he was up here. Too bad. She was beginning to enjoy her own thoughts and hoped he wouldn't have the guts to show up.

"Ghosts? You think 'there are ghosts in here?" She spoke, her face a little lighter than this afternoon, eyes less puffy, and no tears. Perhaps his tirade earlier had helped after all and that was why she was here, deep down hoping to talk to him some more.

"Only good 'uns. I mean just look at this place. It reeks of spirits, writers galore, many dead, and even those are probably pondering their next book. Some literary great like *Left Me in the Wind*, a sequel where he did give a damn and falls in love with the housemaid. Or *Bridges of Jefferson County*, the modern day version of the story where a traveling camera guy realizes he needs more pixels on his digital camera and falls in love with the blonde at the photo shop, only she's into bondage and leaves him tied up in a hotel room. Or even *Frankenstein's Monstrous Inventions*, tales of organic experiments gone wildly wrong, in XXX, of course. Wouldn't want to watch your kids viewing drooling cauliflower cohabitating with lecherous broccoli."

Leanne laughed out loud for the first time, smearing away tatterings of bitterness and loneliness still clinging to her. *He's on a roll and he hasn't had any wine yet. Could be a long night and who knows where it will go?* That roguish curl to his lips tempted her. It wasn't two a.m., but one of those nights when she could use the company and any warm body would do when all she had was Collette's book to curl up to in her room. Who knew if his wife looked decent—maybe she could join as well?

"Are you a writer?" she asked, curious why he would be here otherwise? He had the artistic bent of someone on the edge of madness or ingeniousness.

"No, I was born a little more dexterous than that. Spent most of my life changing spark plugs and oil. They do say mechanics have great hands. As for books and writing, I'm more of a reader. I believe for every great book ever written there's got to be someone or several someones to read it. Or at least someone to appreciate great literature and clutch the covers after they've read the last page and say something profound like, 'Damn good book. So good, in fact, if I was stuck out in the woods with no toilet paper and had to do a number two, I'd use my fingers instead of these pages. It's that good.'"

Leanne made a disgusted grin, and let laughter adorn her face like bridal lace as she chucked her wine back. "Your wife doesn't mind you talking to other women?"

"Oh, chatting is okay, but if the talk turns to baseball and getting to third base, she gets a might cranky. No, at my age, cheering a beautiful woman up and making her blossom like a gorgeous flower is about as close I'm going to get to opening any of your rose petals I'm afraid. The younger generation only thinks of sex, sex, and sex. I once got slapped in a fast food joint for saying lovely pair of buns to the waitress picking up her burger tray. Nobody appreciates good, well-rounded food these days. I tell ya."

Leanne giggled, and excused herself to get another glass of brewed wine. A mechanic, she remembered the time when Jake Cromer paid her to make out on the hood of his rare 1969 Dodge Charger as part of the deal to buy his house. That was erotic, filling other people's fantasies. Something very powerful about that, she thought, maybe it filled part of her creative urges? Trying to invent unique ways of making people happy?

He watched her return, and if she didn't know better he was sizing her up. She wondered what he'd be like in bed. Either a very consummate lover or the exact opposite, quite happy with himself getting his rocks off and leaving her high and dry.

"I think this is more you. Laughing, enjoying life, chatting up older, more mature and debonair men like me, over wine. But if I can ask, your ex? What happened? He absconds with the nineteen-year-old buxom next-door neighbor from the local Hooters restaurant? Turn raving gay, or offed himself in the garage by leaving the car running? I was never great at being delicate about death, or splitting up, but how can you really approach the subject with etiquette? Or maybe he died while walking the dog across the street hit by a…"

"Car crash, the cause was a driver texting. He cut

Ben, my husband, off on the highway and created a five-car pileup. Oddly enough, the driver lived, while my man died in the aftermath. It's why I'm here, trying to get on with my life and in addition to that, my father passed away the same morning." Tears threatened at the thought of him trapped, the car burning, him all busted up and mangled, all because some ass had tried to message, *Hey dude, let's check out that new movie with the crazy turtles flinging themselves around like from some Kung-fu film*, she found out later from the police.

"Texting, don't believe in this new woo-woo technology. They call it communication, but it actually cuts you off from everything outside of yourself. Puts your focus into a little two-by-three box."

She never thought of it like that. "I always wanted to come back here with him. He hated the idea of being in a place without TV, etc. Now I'm here on my own. Starting out all over again, I'm afraid." She pursed her lips. *All those years stolen by some self-centered twit.*

"So you've come to bury his memory or at least pitch it into the sea and let the surf angels take him away to the sun-catchers."

"Never thought of it like that, I suppose you're right. How do you know so much?"

"Been around a bit. My skateboard is on its third set of wheels."

"Or a long childhood," she quipped back. "Look, you make me laugh and that's quite a gift to this sad woman who was pretty angry with you earlier." She stopped and looked at him funny. "Surf angels? How funny—never viewed waves in that way. You sure you're not a writer? Probably could be, your words roll off your tongue with eloquence, wisdom, and a touch of sardonic humor."

"Yeah, that's the third glass of hot wine talking, makes you appreciate illusions in a better light. Laughter is good medicine, cheaper than Viagra, and burns more calories than frowning. Usually makes for better pictures as well. But it's late and I must check up on my wife Cynthia. She's probably still at the Irish pub telling rude Irish jokes or chasing leprechauns, or ruder Irish men." He bowed to her.

Leanne stared at him, lips plump, eyes wide with desire. He stared back, those moments in the movies when the stars glitter and align, the manna in heaven does funny little curly flip-flops in your heart and you do the unthinkable and move in to share a kiss.

As if reading her mind, he looked at her long and hard, pausing. "You know if I was Rhett Butler or Austen's Willoughby or Bridget's Cleaver, I'd reach behind your head, pull you to me, and kiss those waiting lips. Unfortunately, I was born a gentleman. I'm sorry and must bid my fond adieus and go find my whisky-besotted wife or heavens forbid I might do something I'd regret in the morning."

She groaned inside, even a kiss would be good right about now. A single kiss to know she was desired and wanted. "Wait! You said a minute ago something about the sun-catchers. Are they those?" She pointed to the ceramic suns, etched with native designs, dangling in the corner of the library.

"Yes. The little sun-shaped ceramics you see hanging around here. Me. I take them to be the opposite of the dreamcatchers of native beliefs. These give you dreams and instill the faith to grow better things in your life. Or at least cheer you up with positive karma. I guess they give a little sunshine out to those who need it. Hey, maybe they also give you fantastic writing thoughts. Like, man, after I leave here I'm going to starve myself living off only Can Hardly Soup for weeks on end and write insanely like a madman."

"Don't you mean canned hearty soup?"

"Nope, soup so good I can hardly stand it." He cracked an ear-to-ear grin.

Leanne laughed, choking slightly on the wine. "I really fell for that one. Thanks, Tom, for cheering me up." She reached her hand out and shook his, knowing he was leaving in the morning, as was she. He let his hand linger for a moment too long, the look, the knowing glazing his vision. She knew he wanted to crush those dastardly lips to hers. That was good enough for now—that thought alone comforted her. Knowing someone wanted, perhaps hungered for her.

"You're welcome. Some of my stuff is kinda hooky, but then so am I. The wine has wiped me out, and I'm not much for breakfast. I'm a late-morning type of guy, kinda like get out of bed around two p.m. and see what the day drags in. I leave it to others to kick-start it. So good night. But do remember this. They say even deep hurt is temporary, while madness is a lifetime sentence. Just ask Van Gogh or Picasso. Only madness or insanity doesn't hurt as much, unless of course you're trying to express or find yourself. Then there just isn't enough canvasses to paint or watercolors to suffice."

He left her pondering, watching one of the sun-catchers twirl as the heating kicked in and the waves set a dull thunder in the darkness outside. How could he know she wanted to be a painter? She wanted to know what it would be like to never have enough canvasses to express herself. Hopefully, that would change after her classes in Banff. Sighing to the collected ghosts, venerable writers, and spirits assembled to gaze at her plight, she wandered back to her room. "So I guess it's just Collette and me tonight. Damn, a little company would have been nice." Hell, for all she cared, his wife could have joined.

****

Leanne yawned as she set down her book and sipped away at her wine, the bottle of Chardonnay nearly empty. The last one of the Collette series had grabbed her attention, *Claudine and Annie*. She'd been reading it for the last hour or so. It was odd. There was something content about being on the edge of the ocean, with the waves crashing outside and just the book to indulge in. No distractions, here at the end of the known western world.

The book had grabbed her, about a woman, very dominate, that had come to stay with Collette and her husband. That thrilled Leanne—she wasn't into women before she met Sam at the lingerie store. To be seduced by her, controlled and dominated, was a definite turn-on. She enjoyed being the submissive one when it came to females. A hand stole between her legs. What she'd give to have Sam here now. Commanding her. Memories of the night in Sam's lingerie store, being seduced, introducing Leanne to the pleasures of all female sexuality. Leanne never knew she'd have enjoyed it that much and half the fun was telling Ben about it and how aroused he'd gotten.

Propped up against her pillow, soft light on, the world outside faded away. Just her and Collette as the surf crashed, the moon ghosted among the clouds, wine releasing all tensions of the outside world.

As she continued to read, the pages blurred and soon the book fell into her lap.

"Ah, my young American cousin, Leanne. I see that you've fallen asleep with one of my books in your lap."

Leanne blinked. Dark-haired Collette with her mass of curls and sweet smile, reached for the novel and placed it back on the nightstand. Leanne's blouse to her nightgown was half undone, her nipples were erect and her hand rested between her legs where she had been stroking herself. Pleasuring herself, slowly, as she fell asleep.

Collette took a look at her hand. "I see that the book has excited you, *oui*?"

"No, I was just reading," she lied.

"Let us see, my dear." Collette pulled her hand up and held it to her nose. Leanne tried to yank it back, but the older woman held it tight. "Ah, a very musky scent. That of a woman aroused. One I quite enjoy myself on occasion. You were excited. Here, let me clean those for you." With that, Collette flicked her tongue across Leanne's palm and sucked one of her fingers between her lips.

Leanne again tried to pull away, to no avail as the wet mouth stirred something inside. This was wrong, so wrong, so why did it excite her?

The French writer was much stronger. "*Oui*, very tasty." She savored each finger, sucking on them slowly, one by one. Her mouth wet and hot, Leanne quivered as a jolt of desire seared its way through her. This was wrong, another woman, the mistress of the summer school her parents had sent her to, should not be stimulating her, but she was.

The older woman continued to suck away at her fingers. "Ah, I see you enjoy my mouth and tongue on your flesh. Do you not?"

It was Leanne's first summer abroad. Her parents had sent her out to France to meet the famous Collette, who was running this school before she entered college. Collette was perhaps in her late thirties, which to the eighteen-year-old seemed an eternity away. Did her parents know she also had many lesbian affairs? Is that why they sent her?

"So, my dear, my husband, Willy, is away tonight on business and sucking on those fingers has made me quite…how do you Anglo's say…randy."

Leanne felt the stir between her legs. Was this older and stronger woman going to have her as her lover? If she did there was very little she could do about it. Alone in the room, just like the book, she shivered inside. Hers if she desired, Leanne quivered under her lust-filled stare.

"Now, I am going to join you in bed, move over, *ma cherie*."

With that, Collette pulled her gown over her head. Her breasts swung, hanging full. But it was the thick, black hairy patch between her legs that held Leanne's attention. Her own lips tensed. Her own pubic hair had begun to grow, sparse compared to her headmistress's thick controlling looking bush. Would hers look like that soon?

The sight of her first female pubic area, other than her own, excited Leanne. So grown up, so full, so strong and dominant looking.

A thrill ran through her. What if she was forced to bury her face in that forest of pleasure? What if she wouldn't have to be forced? She knew then and there that she wanted to have sex with another woman, at least once.

Who knows, maybe Collette had placed the books here in her room on purpose? Written seduction, hoping it would turn her on. Give her an excuse to seduce her?

"Now, let me help you with yours," she said firmly with her French accent.

Leanne knew now that no was not an option. "I'm still a virgin, I haven't…"

"Ah, but you will. I have something we can use later to deflower you, my dear."

Leanne gasped as Collette removed her gown and slid into bed next to her, both naked. What could she possibly have to do in place of a man?

Leanne shivered as the heat of Collette's body ran up against her. Her softness rubbed against her, the cushiness of her breasts and the coarseness of her pubic hairs rubbing on Leanne's leg. She was entering an area until now she'd never experienced or dreamed existed.

"Now, relax, we have all night. Am I to assume you are inexperienced in the lovemaking between two women, and I'm to presume with a man as well?"

"I've only kissed a boy on the cheek."

Collette's eyes lit up, as they looked Leanne up and down, devouring her with the lust brewing within her, before pulling the covers over them. One hand caressed Leanne's stomach and thighs. "Such a waste of such wonderful young flesh." Leanne tensed as her headmistress's hand ran softly down her thigh. "Now with men, the act of lovemaking can be over in mere minutes. When it comes to women, sometimes the morning comes far too early. That is the beauty, *oui*."

She pulled Leanne's face to hers. "First we kiss. Slow, sensual. I will show you, like this."

Her lips brushed softly over Leanne's. Lips that had kissed many women in her time, were now kissing Leanne. She closed her eyes as Collette's lips fluttered over hers, along her cheek, and against her ear. Hot breath cascaded against her resolve, awakening desire and all of its sensual cravings.

She could feel the hardness of Collette's nipples and the pillowy softness of her breasts against hers as Collette held her face. Leanne couldn't pull away from the delicious feel of breasts on breasts, submitting to the light rain of kisses on her face. She shuddered as Collette's hot breath ran into her ear again, before leaving a slightly moist trail back to her lips. A trail of moisture, leaving a path of drying hunger, arousing her. Collette stopped and whispered softly, "Now do the same to me."

"I've never…"

"Ah, you will and by the end of tonight, I shall have trained you in the art of making love to another woman. We will have many nights after this in which to exhaust each other." She kissed Leanne harder on the lips as she held her head with one hand. Her tongue flicked out to taste the moisture on Leanne's. "Now, do as I did to you."

She stared at Collette, the hunger in her eyes evident. Leanne leaned into her and kissed her in the same light feathering kisses. On her lips, chin, along her ear. Her breath hot in Collette's ear, she licked at her ear. Collette moaned and gasped. "You are a very good learner, I am so aroused for you."

Leanne continued along her neck, leaving light moist kisses. It was a thrill. She'd never excited someone before, enough to want them to crave her.

"Excellent, your kisses are sending shivers through me. I think you are beginning to enjoy this. No?"

Leanne knew the look in her eyes gave her away. She was, as perverse as that thought was. This shouldn't be happening, at least not with another woman and her headmistress, of all people.

"Now, I shall be the teacher and you shall be my obedient student. Agreed?"

"Yes, Miss Collette. I hope to do well in my lessons and impress you."

"Now, that is like music to my ears. I shall strive to be the best teacher you've ever had. One you will not ever forget."

She pushed Leanne back into the pillows and leaning into her, kissed her harder. Taking her lips in desire. Letting Leanne know how much she wanted her. Lips crushed against her young mouth. Her strong tongue invaded her, thrusted against Leanne's. Waves of pleasure flooded Leanne, this woman's lust transmitted through her mouth into the young student. Taking her with her tongue, dominating her.

They kissed for long minutes before Collette broke away, Leanne was virtually panting. She wanted more, she needed to be taken, however that looked, her adolescent female hormone's kicking into overdrive. Leanne opened her eyes, lost in the passion of her kisses, so controlling, so wonderful.

Is this what adults, her parents did at night?

"Now, you do the same to me. Show me your

desire, the hunger that is beginning to flow through you." Collette leaned backward into her pillows.

Normally Leanne would be too shy to take control, but the strange throb between her legs shoved that aside. She moved herself on top of Collette, breasts crushed together, hard nipples drilling into each other. Her pubic area rubbed against Collette's involuntarily. Collette spread her legs, allowing Leanne to nest between them and wrapped them around the youngster.

She kissed the awaiting teacher, letting her overheated senses take control and release herself to the world of sybaritic pleasure. Her lips crushed against Collette's, her tongue invading, like the older lady had done earlier, spearing her way into her wet wanting mouth. Controlling her, time in abeyance as they kissed deeply. She could feel the wetness oozing out of her. The softness of being naked against a woman— thrilling. Softness of breasts crushing into hers, she felt Collette thrust toward her and she responded as her hot mouth hungrily accepted her tongue. Sucking on it.

Collette pulled her head away, finally. She was flushed. "You are either a very good learner or very excited, and you are greatly arousing me."

All Leanne knew was, she wanted this to continue. Never had she felt anything this pleasurable, this stimulating. "And you, me. Or is it that you are an excellent teacher when it comes to making love between women." She panted, wanting to continue— hunger took over any rationality. She'd played with herself, but the lust was never this strong. A craving that cried for more.

"Let's say I've had a fair share of women in my bed and none have left unsatisfied." She smiled, kissing

Leanne sweetly on the lips.

"Then I look forward to the rest of lesson, coming from such an experienced mistress on the subject."

Collette moved Leanne over until they were side by side. She stole her hand down between Leanne's legs and stroked the mound. Her finger dipping into her wet labia. "Now, I want you to do the same to me as I do to you."

Leanne slid her hand between Collette's legs. Slickness answered the call of her probing fingers. Both moaned into the other's mouth as they kissed, their fingers worked in unison stroking each other's vaginas.

"Lightly, my dear," Collette groaned, "and slow."

Collette alternated between sliding her fingers into the wet valley and rubbing over the hood of Leanne's clit. Back and forth, Leanne fell into the pleasure of being masturbated, while she did the same as Collette's kisses stole away her nativity.

They continued for many minutes until Leanne could feel a pressure building from the heat within. Intense arousal, like mini firecrackers began to set off inside her. Explosions erupting, she moaned over and over into Collette's mouth. Her back arcing at the fingers playing into her first orgasm. The urge to scream in release, her fingers strummed her clit like an experienced Cellist, coaxing unknown tunes out of her young body. Notes of sybaritic arousal that she never knew existed within her flared into life.

Leanne put one arm around Collette, trying to hang on as her teacher's tongue drove into her. Finally, she had to release her lover's tongue and suck at her neck. Wracking waves of intensity convulsed through her. Kaleidoscopes of colors misted through her. Her own voice cried out, hoarse with pleasure. Surrendering everything to her mistress' fingers, strumming wave after wave of convulsing delight between her legs. Finally, Collette began to convulse as well and Leanne continued strumming her fingers over the woman's clit until she cried out, "*Mon Ami*," shuddering beside the younger woman, still shivering in her own pleasures.

They both fell back, gasping, and said nothing for a long moment. "So how was that lesson, my dutiful student?"

Leanne kissed her teacher's neck and whispered into her ear, "The most incredible, intense experience I've ever had."

"Well, perhaps the next lesson will also astonish you as I promised I'd do earlier."

Leanne had long forgotten those words and, at the moment, didn't care. She could do anything to her as long as it meant more of the intense explosions. If this was what it meant to make love, she was open to learning whatever Collette would throw at her.

Collette oozed her way out of the bed and slowly padded over to a dresser. Leanne watched her rear jiggling. Did it seem odd that a woman's figure was stimulating? Especially her headmistress'.

Collette pulled out a leather harness and strapped it around her midsection, putting a section between her legs. When she turned around, Leanne couldn't believe her eyes. She bore a large cock, jutting erectly from her.

"Now, my dutiful student, this teacher is to release you fully from the bonds of youth and blossom you into the realm of adulthood. Are you ready?"

"But…" She hesitated. Was she not supposed to remain virginal until her wedding, or at least her one special lover took her or at least a male, her husband?

"No buts, open your legs. I shall be gentle, more so than any man shall."

She was right, Collette was her special lover. The one she would never forget, the one that took away her virginity. There was no other she wanted to have it with.

The elder slowly got on the bed and mounted herself over the prone Leanne. She felt the hardness of her cock at the entrance to her pussy. Collette grabbed both of Leanne's hands and intertwined their fingers as she leaned over and began to kiss her.

The craving to have that hardness overtook Leanne. She wanted Collette to be fucking her, driving her crazy again. Slowly, the thickness of her cock moved into her, and a sharp pain tore at her. Collette held her and temporarily halted her entrance.

"It's okay, that passes. Then true pleasure begins." *Begins? What was the last hour or so all about?*

She moaned as Collette's hardness entered, filling her being. Never in her wildest dreams did she believe she'd be deflowered by another woman, let alone by one of the last century's brilliant lesbian writers.

Collette thrust back and forth. Leanne wrapped her legs around the older woman, allowing her to slowly begin fucking her into the beginnings of senselessness. She drew her lover's cock even deeper into her as Collette stole kisses from her lips. She gripped her by her rear, demanding Collette to drive deeper, harder into her as consciousness slipped away and another orgasm began to send waves like the ocean pounding through her.

With that, Leanne awoke, a smile on her face, the

place between her legs soaked as she got up to use the bathroom. The sun had begun to cut through the morning mists. "Wow, talk about a good book."

Worn out by her erotic dreams, she trundled back into bed and watched the sun cutting away the darkness. She smiled to herself, satisfied for the first time in the last couple of months. *Now, I understand why they say reading books is good for you.* She thought as she packed up her bags. *I've got to search the local bookstore for some more of Collette's books.* Looking in the mirror, a smile graced her lips as she got up and brushed her auburn hair. It was probably the dream of Collette having her, taking her, or was it Tom? He made her laugh last night. Did he awaken a hunger within her that had gone unsatisfied for far too long? She read recently that loneliness did strange things to your soul. Leanne dressed slowly. Before leaving she knew she must thank Tom—he did say this was his last night here. She had originally perceived him as some arrogant ass, but the man had managed to work her through a lot of the pain inside. There was some ray of hope for her, she knew now.

She perused the gift shop next to the front desk before leaving. "I'm checking out now a bit early." She interrupted the porter listening to last night's baseball highlights in a small room adjacent to the desk. Tom was right about the porter's obsession with baseball.

"Damn! Mariners lost again." He shut off the TV in the private room and came out to attend to Leanne, closing the door behind him. "Sorry about that, not supposed to let guests know I've got a TV here. Screw the owners, I don't really care. We're talking important stuff. It's the playoffs." He glared at her. "Was everything all right? Was your stay okay? Which room?"

"Yeah, great. The Claudine room. Say, are there any more of the sun-catchers for sale or have you sold them all? There were a few out here last night. Don't see any for sale this morning."

"What the hell you talking about, lady? We've never had any—damn." He stopped and looked hard at her. "Old guy, dark green suit jacket, khaki pants, and red woolly socks?"

"Lacks fashion sense, yes, that's Tom. He stayed in the Amy Tan room."

"Ah, crap. We keep trying to flush him out every other year, but he keeps coming back, like locusts."

"What do you mean, every other year? How long has he been coming here?"

"Since the forties, I'm told."

"What? That's impossi—he and his wife Cynthia stayed in the Amy Tan room last night. I talked to him, she spent the night at the Irish pub."

He stared blankly at her. "Lady, no one stayed in that room last night."

"No. You're lying." Leanne threw down her luggage and stormed up the stairs. *This is not possible.* The door to the room was open and the bed was neatly made. "How?"

Shelley, the cat, meowed, lifting her head from the middle of the bed where the sunlight was streaming in and glinted off dust specks swirling in the air. No luggage was present, and the bathroom was empty. Everything, the towels, neatly folded, even the end of the toilet paper, shaped into a triangle. Leanne closed her eyes. *How?*

In the hallway outside, no ceramic suns hung. She ran quickly up the stairs to the third-floor library. None hung there either.

Leanne weakly staggered back down the stairs. In the dining room, a lady was cleaning up the cups and setting more coffee for the morning breakfast. "Do you work here?" The older lady nodded back. "Sorry, stupid question time. But have you seen any of the sun-catchers for sale?"

The matronly lady blinked several times. "No, we don't sell such things and never have."

Leanne walked numbly away and waited as the porter finished with another guest at the front desk. She paid quietly as the older lady came down the stairs and pulled the porter aside. "Did she?"

"Yeah, in the Tan room this time."

The lady glanced over at her. "Sorry, you're probably wondering what the hell is going on. I'm the owner here since the 1980s, and James here is correct. Legend has it that one of the earliest writers put a sun-catcher up in the library. I've heard people say they've seen them around over the years. I haven't, then I guess I never needed one. Not bad things, they seem to give people hope and life before they leave. Is the old man Tom with a wife named Cynthia who hangs out at the Irish pub?"

"Yes?"

"Cynthia is his dog's name. He used to go for walks with her out on the beach. I was told he died in the early forties. Sorry. All of my guests here say he's a nice guy, usually makes them happier chatting with him. Good day." She walked back up the stairs.

Leanne stood stunned. He seemed so real. She

touched him, even. He made her cry, laugh, pissed her off. She stood completely still, feeling as if her senses were being slowly drained away, leaving her unable to react.

"You okay?" the porter asked, as another guest arrived to check out behind her.

"Yeah." She breathed in deeply several times to ground herself, and looked down, counting to three. "I'm good." She grabbed her luggage and walked out into the morning sun, as it cast its warm blanket over her. *Too bad, really. If he kept talking and prying me with more wine, he might have got a homerun out of it. One of the true gentlemen left in the world.* She laughed and stared at the beach one last time. *Much unlike the denizens of some of the books around here.*

An old man was walking on the morning sands, his back to her. He stood studying the lighthouse on the cove next to them in the mists. His white dog ran madly about trying to catch the seagulls. She watched the gulls squawking away tormenting the frustrated canine as he tried desperately to catch them.

"Tom would probably say something silly right now like, old Cynthia, thank God she doesn't have any wings, or otherwise she'd end up in Japan chasing dragons. Well, small ones, anyways, before they grew little Bic lighters in their throats and burped hellfire after eating spicy burritos. Crap! His humor is rubbing off on me. Oh, I hope this doesn't mean I'm going to cut off one of my ears and begin writing like mad. I actually hate canned soup." She laughed out loud. "See you, Tom, and thanks for that butt-kicking. You were right, I sure needed it."

Dreaming of being seduced by Collette helped, as

well. *Maybe that along with Tom has helped me to begin working my way through my grief. Well, Sam did say to expect the unexpected. This journey so far had surely proven that, having intimate conversions with a ghost and losing my cherry to Collette in my dreams. Wonder what could possibly happen next—they do say you can't write this stuff, that reality is far stranger than fiction.*

The line of surf angels thundered its reply and the old man in the distance lifted his arm waving offhandedly over his shoulder as if over the ocean's drone he heard her and returned his thanks.

Overhead, the hotel's sign creaked on rusted hinges as the sun began to scatter the morning mist. The smell of hibiscus and roses from the small garden at the entrance to the hotel filled her nostrils. *The open road beckons and it looks like it's going to be a beautiful day for a drive after all. I've got to thank Maureen for mentioning this place.*

Chapter Three

Leanne sat on the cedar-paneled patio of the Wayside restaurant overlooking Cannon Beach. The Haystack rocks that were in all of the world famous photographs of the beach, towered out of the water, and the ocean crashed in silent tribute to the sheer romantic beauty of the place. Gulls and eagles squawked and preened in the background, oblivious to the serene majesty nature had set out on display for the romantic couples that strolled the sands today. Of which she wasn't currently a part of, sadly. Why hadn't Ben and she come here? Was life too short to take time out to enjoy this beautiful place and reflect? A tear streamed down her cheek. Apparently it was and it had taken his death to make her realize that.

She had wanted to drive further up the coast, all the way to the top of Olympic Peninsula, and maybe even take the Blackball ferry over into Victoria, British Columbia, today. Only the view of the rocks was so awe-inspiring, she decided to take a short walk along the beach. *No, I think I'll hang out here for the night. Catch the rocks under moonlight, walk the beach at night. Maybe find myself some young stud-muffin or a woman in need of more than just cuddling.*

A very handsome younger waiter approached her. He was probably early twenties, square-cut jaw. Worked out judging by the squeeze of his short sleeves and the hard line of his rear she caught moments earlier. The dark wavy hair and darker brown eyes caught her gaze as he stood before her. When he smiled there was just a hint of a dimple and a twinkle in his eye. The square-cut jaw and his darker complexion gave him that dangerous, fun-loving look. Like some hunky dude looking for a hot pickup in a bar.

"Hi, I'm Colin, your waiter tonight." He smiled, his young man's eyes eating up the curve of her blouse. His gaze rested a moment too long at her cleavage. She should have been appalled but wasn't. Someone that young giving her the eye was rather uplifting, and she needed all the encouragement she could get these days.

She grinned back. "Leanne. I'll have a glass of Chardonnay first before I order, if you don't mind. I thought I'd sit here and enjoy the view."

"So many do. Take all the time in the world." He stared back at her, liking what he saw, she could tell in the subtle opening of his iris. Something she had learned to watch out for when showing a home to a potential buyer. There was something wonderful in being admired, especially by a hunk of a young virile-looking male, whose eyes told her they liked what they had seen and she didn't mind it at all.

Leanne got lost again in the view of the rocks as he sauntered up.

"Your wine, Leanne. Yes, many come here for the view. I have to agree it is stunning, extremely romantic and very seductive." His voice lowered to a deeper huskiness, snaring her attention from the natural sights just outside.

Leanne turned, his eyes were devouring her. She decided to tease him and slowly crossed her legs, letting the dress slide a little up her leg.

"Sorry," he choked, blushing. "I meant the view of the beach."

She caught him red-handed at her slight implied gesture. His gaze took a moment too long again, lingering on her thighs and the thrust of her cleavage, before meeting her eyes. Leanne smiled to herself—at least she could turn the head of a young stud like him.

A little before the dinner rush would begin, the place was nearly empty. But other than the special breakfast they did every morning at the Nye Beach Hotel as part of the stay there, she hadn't eaten all day, preferring to just drive, hit all the parks and seaside stops. Loving the views of this state, she wondered why she and Ben had never done the Oregon coast. The wine was already hitting her head on her empty stomach.

"Yes, sorry." He smirked. "I got to be honest, for a woman older than me, I do find you rather more stunning than the view out there," he blurted out.

Oh, the impetuous of youth. "Thanks, I appreciate the frankness." A weak smile tread her lips. "So, I'll be blunt back." She knew she shouldn't say this, but other than having intimate conversations and orgasms with ghosts, she was starving for a little conversation and company. "Am I in what your age group would call a milf?"

His eyes widened, giving him away before he responded. "No, well yes, to be truthful. Ah, look, I'm sorry I shouldn't be hustling a customer. I've got to get to my other table. Sorry, again. But you are indeed very gorgeous. Are you waiting for your husband to arrive before ordering?"

"No, I'm not married, widow, actually. Just decided to shake off my melancholy and do something for myself. Thought I'd do a road trip, go up the coast, and perhaps go into Canada. I think I'll order now, Colin. I'd like to try the Prawns Scampi, what do you think?" She crossed her legs again, teasing him. He lowered his notepad slightly, catching the slow cross of her legs. Either it was the wine, him, or the romantic nature of the setting, but Leanne was starting to feel very aroused. There was something very sexy in turning a man on with the sight of her body. Especially someone as young and handsome as him.

"Ah," he stuttered, "there are some views one can never get tired of looking at." He smiled slightly at her. "As for my opinion, the fresh Coho Salmon is far better, caught yesterday by George our Greek ex deep sea diver, with his teeth at thirty feet down and flung, still flapping into ice. Then driven here at six knots per hour under a strong headwind. Waiting for such a beautiful woman as yourself to tastefully enjoy."

Leanne laughed. "Hate to be his wife and have to kiss those lips."

Colin smiled his wonderful full grin on that strong jaw. "Served on a bed of wild rice. We had to fight them into the back of the restaurant, good thing our chef knows some karate. Dirty fighters, they don't call them salmon and rice wild for nothing. So, if you hear any crashing back there, they're still putting up quite the struggle. Also served with braised broccoli drizzled in extra virgin olive oil, and stir-fried with crushed coriander seeds for the veggies on the side. My personal favorite meal."

"And you can vouch for the virgins." She gulped

down more wine, becoming enamored and turned on by this cheeky gorgeous waiter, who was obviously wanting to turn her eye.

"Personally inspected by myself for authenticity and yes, I had to restrain myself from any dalliances. While they were quite pretty, none a match to your natural beauty."

Leanne beamed. "Why thank you, Colin." He was quite the charmer. "I'll have the Coho then, but if I see any teeth marks, it gets sent back."

"Deal. More wine?"

"Sounds good." He walked away. Leanne thought about his honesty and humor. It was flattering to her ego to have a man at least ten years younger desiring her, and not afraid of speaking his mind, let alone making her laugh, which in her current state of mind was a great distraction. He lifted her spirits. Leanne smiled as she sipped at her wine, watching him as he moved with that rare confident grace that some men had. What would he be like…

She ran her finger down her cleavage, imagining him naked on top of her, thrusting into her, as she held on like a rag doll. He'd probably last all of ten minutes, but it would be a good and hard ten. Right about now, that would be exactly what she needed and wanted. Nothing deep and sentimental, just a good thrashing about under the bedsheets.

Colin returned minutes later with her wine. "Leanne, I don't want to be very forward, and if you say no, I won't be offended, but there's something about you that excites me. If you would like some company, I asked my boss and he said I could leave early tonight if there's no real rush in the next hour.

After today, I've got three days off to myself, and I'll be heading back home to Vancouver. I know the coast, Victoria, and the Island well. I could show you around if you'd like some company."

Her tongue caught in her throat. She hadn't expected this. Was she ready to try this? To have a young man with her, who only had one thing on his mind? What would Ben have said under the circumstances if this were him? She knew what Sam would have said, and so far sleeping alone sucked. Not to mention he was quite the looker. "I'd like that. Vancouver? BC not Washington, I imagine."

"Correct, why?"

"Well, would you like me to drive you up the coast? We could have some fun together. I was going to Vancouver before heading inland to Banff for an arts program I'm registered in. It would be cool to check out the Island and Victoria. Could drop you in Vancouver."

He smiled lewdly at her, and she knew he was thinking of a lot more than driving. "I know the coast and Vancouver Island even better, but I'm only a student and a waiter on minimum wage. So I haven't got much to donate financially."

"No worries, it'll be my tab. I just got a huge inheritance, so just call me a rich milf. I pay, you show me around, and I drop you off in Vancouver. Nothing implied or expected."

"I don't know what to say, I'd be honored, I guess." He glanced at her, licking his lips. "So would I be expected to provide you with some, ah, personal services as part of my escorting?"

She smiled back at him. "Would you turn me down if I said yes?"

"Ah, no. I find you very attractive. It'll be very hard to keep my hands off you, but it's your tab so I'll be a true gentleman at whatever disposal you like. Would you like another glass of wine, while you wait for me? Give me about an hour or so, and if it doesn't pick up, I'm all yours. Enjoy the view and the meal."

Leanne looked him up and down, doing the same thing he did to her when he first saw her. "I will." She coyly watched him as he waited on the other table and a third as another couple came in. The ripple of muscle as he lifted plates. The outline of his well-shaped rear—he obviously worked out or at least did some kind of sports. Yeah, crazy or not, she could use the company. Virile male company. He seemed sincere and if this lead to anything, it would be a bonus. If nothing else, someone just to talk to would be more than great. Watching couples in love on the beaches wasn't cheering her up.

He smiled warmly at her as he walked past. Who was she really kidding? By the look in his eyes, it would definitely lead somewhere, and that would definitely be more than okay. More like damn welcomed.

A little more than an hour later, Leanne had finished her meal. He was right, it was very good, along with a third glass of wine. The crowd, as anticipated, hadn't grown much larger. Colin walked up with an ear-to-ear grin. "I'm yours for the next week. I can catch the Amtrac on Tuesday to get back to work like I sometimes do. Just got to pack a few things. I live up the street in an apartment with a couple of guys. Meet you on the beach in half or so?"

"By the rocks. I'd love to walk as a couple along

the sand. Seen so many others strolling, holding hands, laughing, would be a nice memory." Company and someone to talk to besides the chatter in her own head, would be more than nice, even a hand to hold on the beach at this point would be fantastic. But judging by the bulge in his slacks, she could hold something harder than his hand.

"Deal." He leaned in and kissed her on the cheek. "Can't wait, my darling milf. Colin P. James at your service in whatever desire you require." He bowed and gracefully swept his hand at her like in the movies.

Leanne blushed. "You really okay with having a rich older lady taking care of you? I've got to be honest, I'm a bit nervous; I've never done anything like this before."

"Well that makes two of us. I shall endeavor to richly reward your experience these next few days in every way you feel comfortable doing and attempt to reward your experience up the coast with my witty conversational charm."

"In every way?"

"In every way, you would like. Leanne, I really do find you very attractive, sexy, really. Always wanted to date a redhead. So I'm your male escort, in as far as you want to go." He took her hand and kissed it as they strolled out of the restaurant.

She knew exactly where he wanted to go and it didn't involve reciting Shakespeare or pointing out the strata of the ocean rocks.

"Thank you. I appreciate the sincerity. And if I get emotional, I apologize now, it won't be because of you."

"I understand, don't know what it's like to lose a

significant other, and hope I don't have to. Oh, there's one thing I won't do. I hate getting sand in my butt. So no wild kinky stuff on the beach."

Leanne laughed. "Then you've obviously had wild kinky sex on the sand to know how it feels."

"Yeah, guilty as charged." He smiled richly and kissed her on the lips quickly. "Back in a flash."

She patted him on the rear as he turned away. "Don't worry, my good man. I'll make sure we get a blanket to protect that great-looking, tender ass of yours." Leanne giggled as he briskly strolled away. Oh, this had better be a good idea. It was certainly the craziest thing she ever tried. Still, he seemed very sincere, and she was a good judge of character. Not to mention she knew where he packed his sandwiches, judging by the heavy bulge in his slacks and the lust in his eyes.

****

The moon rising behind the clouds and the monolithic Haystack rock caught her breath. It was a warm night, the sun just beginning to set, and a few people still strolled the beach. Leanne felt sad and happy at the same time. She was going to take a perfect stranger with her for the next few days. Was this what they called rebound? Or just some way of getting herself to feel better inside while trying to get over Ben's death? Or just some casual shag, and did it really matter at all?

All she knew was she hadn't gotten used to sleeping alone in bed yet, their bed. She'd have to get rid of it when she got back and get a new one that didn't bring back memories of Ben. She sent a text to Janice to tell her to do that, along with the message.

—Meeting hot young stud on Cannon Beach.—

Janice replied. *—Now you're talking. Have lots and lots and lots of fun. Oh, should I make that a single or a double and should I make sure there's a place to attach handcuffs?—*

—For me or him?—

—LOL—

A wolf whistle broke her texting as Colin came striding up. "Seeing you highlighted against the moonlight has most definitely aroused all of my male hormones. You look stunning." He kissed her quickly on the lips. "Like I said, if I'm being too forward, let me know. This is your holiday and I don't want to wreck it by my male ego wanting to make love to you, here and now."

"My, my, you definitely are excited. It's okay. I like the sound of that. Let's go for a walk along the beach first. Hold me. I think there's some privacy over by those rocks, and being the gentleman, carry my blanket I got from the back of my car. I think we'll get rid of some of that male hormone saturation and then we can relax and get to enjoy each other a little more."

"Oh, lady, I like your way of thinking." He grabbed her blanket and held her hand. She loved the warmth of his skin against hers.

As they walked, Leanne asked, "So what makes you work here? Have family in Canada?"

"My dad met Mother in America. She was up here on a work Visa but didn't want to stay forever. So the deal was when the last of the kids left home; me, Mom, and Dad were to return here to retire. Mom's father ran a restaurant here and willed it to them, which made it easy to return. Dad was a chef and had a great sense of business. So I come out here to work the busy summer months and return to Vancouver for my studies. So tell me about you—how does a gorgeous redhead end up in Cannon Beach by herself?"

Leanne caught sight of another couple ahead of them embracing and kissing in the misty moonlight. She leaned into Colin watching him staring at the couple.

"But first," he said as he pulled Leanne to him, "we can't stand out like sour thumbs." His mouth possessed hers, and kissed her as the ocean crashed slowly in the background.

Strong male lips tasted hers. It had been a long time since another man had kissed her besides Ben. She ran her hands up his arms. Sinewy muscles in his arms pulled her in, his lips possessing her, deeply. The rugged male strength held her to him as he continued his kiss. Leanne melted against him, her resolve grinding in complete surrender to his male hardness as they continued kissing. She could feel his hunger for her throbbing against her body. His tongue slow and dominant, probing hers, taking her mouth as he pleased. God, it had been months since she'd been kissed this way, this passionately. Maybe years before Ben even.

A man who hungered for her, needing to take her, have her under him. Inside her. That was what it was like when she and Ben had first met. The passion. Desire peeling away all sense of anything besides them, besides him possessing her. A tear trembled down her cheek as she reacted to his need with her own.

"You okay?" he asked as he pulled away.

"Oh, most definitely yes. It has been many years since I've been kissed with such desire. It reminded me of Ben, my former husband, how much he wanted me, how much I wanted to be the object of his desire." She couldn't believe how she gave in and surrendered to his kiss, how much it aroused her. *It had been far too long, lady. Here, I thought I'd be afraid and back away from his kisses.*

Colin smiled. "Good. I hate getting showed up by another couple. They're probably thinking to get a damn room. I don't know about your other men, but that's what you do to me. Besides, I thought I'd give you something to remember this night by and perhaps ease the pain of his memory a little."

"Oh, you did that." Leanne lifted her face to his and as the tears streamed down, she crushed her mouth to his. Her internal hunger took over, needing him inside her. It was insane how she gave in to him. A stranger, his needs, his wants. Colin craving her. What a turn-on to arouse him, make him want to desire her. He was the best thing of this holiday so far and even better yet, he was real.

Leanne released his rather shocked lips. "We need to act on our passions, but first a selfie for memory's sake, with the clouds, the rocks behind us, and the moon ghosting through."

Both of them took several pictures, each with their own cameras. Colin wrapped his arms around her and kissed her again as they walked arm and arm to the cluster of rocks near the water's edge. Leanne glanced around, there was hardly anyone on the beach anymore. The other couple had left, and the moon ghosted behind a thickening fogbank. Shadows of the rocks darkened the sky and the beach. Mist rolled lightly in to hide them even further.

Colin spread the blanket out on the still warm sand. "You sure you want to do this?"

"Oh, yes. I think we need to get this out of the way so we can enjoy each other's company later in our journey. I was a little hesitant about asking you, but after that kiss. I need relief, and judging by the bulge in your slacks, I think you need the same. Besides, I haven't been kissed with that kind of passion except perhaps by Ben, in my whole life. You've woken that need inside to be taken. I know it's hard for men to understand, sometimes a woman just has to be possessed, wanted, and craved for, more than anything."

"Lady when I first saw you at that table, I said to myself, man I wish I was her husband, because I'd be taking her up to our room and shagging her brains out every night. Oh, and I brought protection." He patted his pocket.

Not exactly the most romantic proposal she ever had, but under the circumstances, any warm body to satisfy would do right about now. She almost wanted to cry inside—was this starting to go past the times spent with Ben. Was she really ready? Trust what Sam told her, 'expect the unexpected', something she had to do in her line of work in order to satisfy her clients. Now she had to do the same to satisfy herself. "I hope you brought a few spares because you've woken up a lot of hunger in this lady and a lot of memories I need to get over." God, this was such an unexpected turn of events.

"Hey, I like the idea of shag therapy. But I don't know anything about you. You've not told me much about yourself." Ben stalled.

Maybe he was nervous, she wasn't sure.

Leanne reached behind her and unbuttoned her dress. It fell to the blanket in a hush. She unsnapped her bra and her breasts jiggled free, nipples hardening in the cool air, as she pulled down her floral panties. "Are you going to talk or are you going to take me here and now? We'll talk later, this trip is my deal, remember."

Colin gulped. "God, you've got an incredible body."

She could see his hardness thrusting against his jeans. Colin hastily yanked his shirt over his head and unzipped his jeans. Leanne caught the sight of his throbbing, hard circumcised cock. The head, purple with blood, he wasn't huge, like in porn-star massive— he had a good seven inches in length and a nice thickness. She wanted to get on her knees and suck on it, but knew if she did he wouldn't last very long. What she really wanted and needed was him inside her, filling that void since Ben had gone. While another woman was great, there was something about a man taking her and making her feel possessed, rivaled everything else.

He slipped the condom over himself, and a slight moan escaped his lips. "Oh, you can't imagine how much I crave you."

"I want this to be as slow as possible, do you think you can manage that?" She sank to the warmth of the blanket, surf resonating by them.

He nodded. "I'll be as slow as possible, but I'll apologize now. I've been without for a while and like you, you've woken up cravings I've kept buried for far too long."

"Well then, I'm going to try to give you something to remember as well." Leanne pulled him to her as they sank onto the blanket. His mouth, hard against her, betraying what he wanted to do as she wrapped her legs around him and slowly pulled the hard cock into her wetness. She was wet even before he kissed her, more so after. She groaned as his hard thickness entered her and like a true gentleman, he slowly filled her. His cock steadily sliding inside. That was what she missed, a man's hardness.

She pulled her mouth away. "God, that feels so damn good." "Slow, kiss me slow, let me do the work at first." He was thicker than Ben and that was such an incredible feeling of being stuffed by such a hard cock. Her dream of being taken by Colette's strap-on did nothing compared to having a real man inside her.

He wrapped his arms around her. Course hairs raked her breasts and nipples, already hard in the cool air. She moved slowly flexing, herself over his rigid cock. She put her hands on his hips. "Rotate your hips like this." Her hands guided him to swivel inside her. He returned to kissing her while rotating his hips slightly. "Now slowly slide forward."

Inch by agonizing inch she felt his cock straining for release inside her. Leanne knew if it wasn't for the thickness of the rubber he'd probably already have exploded.

She ran her hands down his back and sides until they cupped his taut butt. She felt the flex of his muscles in her hands as he began to plunge himself in and out, feeling every inch of him. Her nails scraped his back, her legs wrapped behind his. "Hold still, let me do the work." She slid down his length.

"Wow, this is amazing. So erotic, I've never done it like this," Colin moaned, nearly frozen in his own lust, unable to feel anything but her moving around his throbbing cock. Leanne was doing most of the work, her internal needs catapulting her into that zone of lost pleasure as every nerve ending vibrated. She could feel the shake begin inside.

Leanne wanted to cry out, "Fuck me hard," but didn't. Colin wouldn't last long if he did. That was for another time, or as good as this already felt, later tonight. She sucked on his neck, lost in hunger's sexual grasp as she slid herself along him, working her vaginal muscles, squeezing his cock.

Now it was just about the two wallowing in the delicious feel of them together. Wiping out the remembrance of what Ben was like. Even Ben couldn't do it like this young man could. His mouth possessing her as the waves crashed in the background and mists wavered on stray sea breezes. Leanne felt a surge building within her. Electricity firing nerves, his cock filling her. Usually the slow orgasms were the intense ones, and she knew this one was going to tear her head off.

"Go slow...I'm, oh, gonna come. So fucking fast. You are unbelievable, Colin."

Sweat beaded his brow. "It's all you, lady. I've never, oh God, never done it this slow. It's amazing, like tantric sex. I'll try, I don't know how I've not..."

Was all Leanne heard as she began to thrust herself under him, taking him into her, all the way in. Her will floundered against his virility, the firmness of his young, hard body. Crashing like the ocean waves under his unwavering strength. It was too much as his firmness entered her again and his tongue thrust into her. Leanne cried out, exploding. Holding him, unable to stop herself. Wave after wave of pleasure erupted like a built-up volcano.

He released her mouth and straightened his arms, arching his back. Obviously trying to hang on. "I can't hold it anymore."

"Take me now, as hard as you want." The explosions continued to rip through her.

Colin thrust forward. "Oh," was all that he could muster as she felt his cock grow even harder and convulsions wracked his body. He rammed himself into her again.

His orgasm ripped through him. Even with the condom on, she could still feel him pulsate inside her, leaving him breathless. Spasms thrust through him as he held himself deep within her. Leanne continued to move, thrusting herself onto him, milking him on. Another wave of intensity seared through her as she came again or kept coming it didn't matter, getting lost in the electricity searing through her.

Colin opened his eyes and leaned in to kiss her softly, convulsions still going through him. "That was the most incredible orgasm I've ever had," he whispered into her ear.

"And intense," Leanne whispered back. She sucked at his lip, unable to quell the shakes rippling through her as she continued moving under him. "If you can, stay inside me and don't stop kissing me. Let me do the rest. I'm not done yet."

Leanne continued slowly, sliding on Colin's still-hard cock. Rubbing her g-spot against the edge of his head. With each thrust, another wave of pleasure seared through her. Colin gasped as he probably realized she was coming in one endless wave after another, like the ocean crashing beside them.

Finally Leanne yelled, "Stop." They both panted as he held her in his arms, sweat smearing between them. He moved to get off but Leanne held him tight. "No, stay like this until you go soft, inside me." She needed to be held, loved at this very moment as she slipped away into some state of blissful contentment with him holding her and keeping her warm.

She kissed him and nibbled his ear as she began to return from the boundaries of sensuality. Finally too soft to stay inside anymore, he slipped out and gently rolled off her.

Neither spoke as the mist drifted by, their breaths rising into the air. The ocean waves sent sand sighing along the beach. Only their hands touched as they lay there. Cool air on her skin, evaporating moisture bringing her back from a land of delirium.

Leanne rolled over and curled into his arms. "Wow, didn't expect that. You are totally amazing, Colin."

"Me? Lady, that was the most fantastic lovemaking I've ever had. It was all you, and that is unbelievable. Most of the younger women I've dated are like me, just enjoying a chance to have sex with another person, each sort of just getting themselves off if you know what I mean. By the way, were you having multiple orgasms? Never did that to a woman before."

"Yeah, I just kept coming over and over. Only ever did that once before and it wasn't with a male." She knew right then and there that bringing him along wasn't going to be a mistake. It was exactly what she needed to erase the pain of her past.

"What? Another woman?"

Leanne nodded.

"Now this you better tell me about and more of what brought you here."

"Back at my hotel room, with some wine and I'll see if you're ready for another round. But for now, just hold me." They stared at the dark bulk of the Haystack rocks highlighted against the moon as she snuggled into his arms.

"Okay, when my body begins to regain some semblance of wanting to move." He kissed the top of her head. "Right now, I couldn't even dream of trying to get it hard again, let alone having sex. Never thought I'd ever say that. So safe to say you've been with at least one other woman?"

"Several, I'll tell you in explicit detail. Think that will get you aroused again?" She cupped his balls, already shrinking back into his body from the cool air.

"Oh yeah, always wanted to do a threesome and watch two women going at it." He smirked. "Probably most males' fantasy."

"Who knows, play your cards right and maybe we'll find a woman to join us at some point of our trip."

"You, lady, are completely out of this world. What reality did I disintegrate from and get reborn into my craziest fantasies?" He leaned over and kissed her.

Leanne could feel him already stirring as she continued to massage his testicles. "I think we need to take off the used protection and get you into my room for some more fun." And from what crazy reality did she attract this amazing young stud? The vacation had taken a sudden delicious turn.

Colin rose very slowly, his body limber yet stiff from the cold air and exertions. Leanne smiled. He was already semi-erect. Nothing wrong with having a younger man with her. She liked knowing he was nearly ready to go again. Colin turned around to retrieve his clothes as she struggled to get up. "And look, not even one bit of sand in your butt." She reached over and playfully slapped his firm ass cheeks. They both laughed as they dressed.

****

In her hotel room, they indulged in a steamy shower, his touch leaving a trail of sensations as he lathered her body. As Colin got out, Leanne noticed his hard cock. "I see you're ready to go again." Leanne smirked.

"Well, you tease, you haven't told me about the times you had with another woman. My fantasy mind is going into overload. Was it good?"

"Much better than I ever thought possible. At least women know how to pleasure each other, unlike a lot of men. I once read that a female's idea of a perfect night of lovemaking is perhaps being greeted with roses, taken to a romantic dinner, wine, walking together on the beach. Perhaps kissing and stroking each other in front of a fire. Everything up to the actual penetration…"

"Let me guess—most men's idea of perfection takes over after the intercourse starts."

"Yup, that's about it. Most men think only with their other head. Probably why most women would prefer and are attracted to older gentlemen in their life. They know how to wine, dine, and pleasure their partner."

Colin slipped under the covers with Leanne as they toasted their glasses and sipped at the heady Shiraz. "So since I'm your escort in training, I want to know how to properly pleasure you. Show me what a woman can do to you."

"You really are a wonderful man. Okay, you begin by looking after her needs first. Most men come once perhaps twice and don't last very long once they're inside. So another woman would take her time giving and ultimately receiving pleasure from her partner. Not all women are obviously the same, and we all have our secret fantasies. Some might like to be talked dirty to— not really my thing. Many won't admit it, they like to be taken against their will by their man. You need to ask what it is that turns them on. Most, though, like to be held, kissed endlessly, and played with. Nothing as erotic as having another woman masturbating me as we kiss and I do the same."

"Really, you've done that?"

She could see his cock throbbing under the sheets. Leanne reached under and did a slow stoke to his cock. "You see, with most women, one or two orgasms is just the start. Not all are able to perform multiple orgasms, but many can if the partner is willing to let them or if nothing else one after another."

"Is that why I've been told lesbians can go at it all night?" He kissed her sweetly. Leanne ran her hands along the muscular, sinewy arms. There was something erotic about a man's strong muscles.

"Oh yeah." Leanne reached over and kissed him on the cheek. "And tonight, if my student is willing, I'll show you how."

"I'm a great learner, and I hear practice, practice and more practice makes a perfect lover."

"Now, enough talking, kiss me, and take your time. I'll give you all the queues on what to do. Patience is the key. I know you want to enter me, but the trick is to pleasure me and hopefully make me come first. If you can do that to your women, I don't think they'll throw you out of bed for eating crackers or spilling beer."

They both laughed. "My kind of lessons." Colin turned, keeping himself propped on one shoulder, and slowly kissed Leanne on the lips.

"Listen to what excites her, kiss my neck, lick me there. She'll tell you what excites her in her breathing and gasps."

Colin did, taking his time, running his mouth and lips over her face, along the crook of her neck. Kissing her with wet, soft kisses. His tongue flicked out slowly. Leanne inadvertently moaned. He licked at her ear—she shuddered.

"You like that?" he whispered.

"Yes." She grabbed his hand and put it between her legs. "Now make your way to my breasts with those lips and begin to pleasure my breasts, particularly along the underside, very sensitive there. Stroke me between my pussy lips with your finger. Slow and softly, unlike having your hard cock in me, it is much more intense if you stroke my pussy softly."

He did, his index finger dipping into the moist vee of her labia. She groaned as he licked his way down to her breasts. "Try licking at my armpit—some people are really aroused by it."

He did, again not asking questions as he allowed her to direct him. "Nice, move your lips along the underside of my breasts. Yes, hmmm, like that."

Her nipples were erect. "Lick around the nipple before sucking on it. Some just like to be sucked, for others light bites are a turn-on, usually just before they begin to come. Mild pain can be a great turn-on and stimulating. Softly with your finger." She grabbed his hand to show him. "Rub the tip of my clitoris gently." She shuddered involuntarily as he stroked her perfectly. "Oh, that's very good. Sure there isn't a shred of woman inside you? Take two fingers and trap my clit between them, rub them back and forth."

He did as his mouth continued to lick at her throbbing nipple. He held the throbbing flesh between his lips and nibbled at her.

Searing, lovely pain ripped through Leanne. He was learning perfectly how to arouse her. "Get between my legs. I want your tongue to replace those magical fingers. She lifted her legs and placed them on his back as he got between her thighs. "Now the same, light slow strokes occasionally licking across the nub of my clit."

Colin dipped his hard tongue into her slit, a moan escaping his lips. "Pleasuring your partner can be quite the turn-on, can't it?" She arched her back as he dipped his tongue into the entrance to her pussy.

Another moan escaped his lips in response as his tongue began a slow dance of pleasure along the valley of her pussy.

"That's what women can do to each other. Want to continue?"

He nodded and flicked his tongue over the exposed end of her clit. Leanne bucked in response, lost in the throes of pleasure he was dishing out. Even Ben wasn't this good at oral sex.

"Now, lick down toward my perineum, a very sensitive area for most women and men I'm told. Be brave, lick around my anus and gently fuck me with your tongue. Not all women, obviously like this, but for some it drives them wild." He did, and she grunted in response. "Now not all ladies like being licked there. I do and like I said earlier, by the noises they make, you'll know and if not, ask later."

He moved his tongue back along her perineum and began sucking her pussy lips, before dipping in and fucking her with his tongue there as well. Leanne held the back of his head against her. She sensed the beginning of intensity building. "Now, finish me off, start very softly sucking on my clit and slip a finger or two inside. A lot of women really get off by having, oh God, having their partner lightly suck their clit."

His hot mouth descended on her throbbing clit, begging for release from the torture he instilled in her senses. She shook. "Softer, suck me softer. Oh God, like that. Just like that. Nice and softly. Put your fingers into me." Convulsions began to erupt inside as she held his head to her. Colin's fingers slid inside, one, then two, filling her. "Reach forward with your fingers, find a rough area, and caress it."

Colin stroked her G-spot. Waves of electricity exploded inside. She thrust against his fingers and mouth as he continued to suck on her clit. "Don't stop unless I tell you." She lost herself in her orgasms as he kept pleasuring her.

Colin reached under her with his other hand and slipped a wet finger into her anus. "Oh fuck, great thinking." That was all she could muster as both hands stroked at her like having two cocks inside of her, something Leanne hadn't done yet, but wanted to do someday. Who knows, perhaps it could happen on this holiday yet. Waves of agonizing splendor seared through her. She humped his face, holding it to her wetness until she collapsed into her pillow. "Enough."

Her legs fell limp to his back, and she released her grip on his head. Sweat streamed down her face. Stomach quivered in shudders. "Man, you weren't kidding about being a fast learner. That was better than most of the orgasms women have given me."

He smiled, wiping her moisture from his lips. "I don't want to disappoint you, especially since you seem eager for round two tonight, but this is your call."

"I was going to begin playing with myself, but I knew if I did I wouldn't last long—almost came while I was pleasuring you."

"Put on a condom and sit in that chair."

He moaned, shaking as he quickly unfurled the rubber along his cock. She could see the purple head engorged with blood. It wouldn't take him long. It was obvious he'd enjoyed pleasuring her.

Leanne struggled to rise, limp from her exertions. She'd lost count of her orgasms and, like a lot of guys, just wanted to lie there, relishing the heady aromas of sex and the lassitude it brought after.

She stood up and spread her legs as he sat in the chair. Slowly, she lowered herself onto his rock-hard cock. It filled her insides as she slid down the length and sat on his lap. "Oh, fuck, there's nothing quite like a hard throbbing cock, though." Leanne leaned forward and slid her tongue into his mouth. Her raw nipples caressed against the course hairs of his chest as she began to move.

Colin grunted into her mouth.

"I'd thought you'd like this, very tantric." She flexed her vaginal muscles, clenching his cock and releasing it as she slowly lifted herself. "I'll do all the work. A lot of women like to get on top. They know how to move in order to get the most stimulation, and in this case, I think we'll see if I can get you off as well."

"Oh, that won't take too long. I'm more than okay with letting a woman take control. In fact, I like surrendering, besides it leaves my hands free to fondle you." Too quickly, she felt his cock harden inside her. He was coming in an eruption. Colin held her to him, cupping her ass cheeks in his hands. His legs flexed, his body going ridged as a very intense orgasm seared through him. Hot sperm splashe within the condom. Leanne kept riding him, hoping to have another herself, but as much as she wanted to, she couldn't manage another right away.

She kept riding him, allowing his shudders and spasms to subside. Finally she kissed his ear. "How was that?" she whispered.

"You were so wet, I didn't think I'd last long." He kissed her back, opening his dark brown eyes. "Wow."

"You're an amazing teacher."

"Only because I've such a willing and eager-to-please student." She laughed, kissing him again. "And I do like the hard part." She had definitely made the right choice in picking the young man up for her trip. Ben had never been this good or usually unable to go for a second time like this willing man was.

"Now, I think we can finish off that wine and grab some sleep."

"Who's got the energy to drink after that?" he joked as he held her and kissed her softly. He stood up effortlessly with Leanne still on his lap and his cock inside her and walked over to the bed holding her to him.

Leanne loved having a strong body like his to hold her. Later, if he had the stamina, she'd get him to do her standing up, with her legs wrapped around him.

****

The next day, they drove up the Oregon coast via Highway 101 and stopped in Astoria for lunch. Leanne had always wanted to drive over the Astoria/Meglerbridge, over four miles long and one of the highest cantilever bridges in the world. It was made famous in the *Short Circuit* movie made in the eighties she'd watched as a child. From there, they scouted out several beachside rest stops, caught seals frolicking, seabirds diving and squawking away. Ships in the distance. Other couples holding hands, kissing on the beach.

Finally, he directed her along the Washington coast and they went into the Hoh rainforest at Olympic National Park. She bought some running shoes for them and together they hiked the short Hall of Mosses trail. Sitka spruce and Maples were so covered in ferns and mosses it looked like an old man's beard hanging green and verdant. The rainfall here indeed made it a virtual rainforest with moss and ferns taking over every exposed surface. Nature in all of its lush glory. The pure earthy smells were so grounding. Why hadn't she done this before?

Colin was great company, narrating as much as he could. He knew a lot about the forest, its surroundings, and the rest. He laughed. 'I just read from the tourist brochures.' At one point they caught another couple kissing passionately pressed up against a large moss-covered spruce. His hands were all over the girl, hers rubbing his hardness. The two hadn't spotted them.

Leanne whispered into Colin's ear, "Wow, didn't know that hiking was so stimulating. Ever have sex in the forest?"

"No, other than the other night on the beach, I've lived a rather sheltered life and besides, the ground is quite damp and full of bugs and tiny critters. Don't think you'd really like that."

She massaged the front of his pants. "We'll have to try something different in order to get our rocks off. I'll bet no one's ever done this to you before." She rubbed the front of his crotch. All too quickly she could feel his cock stirring. Leanne unzipped his pants and reached inside to fondle the hardening hot cock. "Shhh, don't let them see us."

She began to expertly stroke his cock. Colin moaned slightly as she kissed him and stroked his cock, feeling it harden in her hand.

The girl was moaning as her man reached into her pants and was obviously masturbating her. She was moaning in pleasure as he fingered her. "I think he took lessons from you on how to pleasure his partner."

"Only because I've a great teacher."

"What's the old saying, for every great teacher, a student comes along, and for every great student a teacher." She smiled at him.

Colin looked softly at her. "I never believed I'd be in the company of an older, very sexy lady. Something intensely erotic about that for me and a redhead. Trust me, you've already reached my quota of bucket-list fantasies."

"Ah, this would be the bonus plan." Leanne sank to her knees and freed his throbbing cock from its confinement. With one hand, she stroked him and began to lick around the engorged head. Opening her mouth, she looked up at Colin as she slid his penis into her wet mouth slowly as far as she could, deep-throating him.

Colin's legs went limp for a second. A slight gasp slipped from his lips as she began to perform fellatio on him.

Leanne softly sucked him in and out, at the same time stroking his cock. She loved the feel of his hardness in her mouth and knew like her clit, too much pressure wasn't good. Colin groaned quietly nearly every time she had him deep in her throat.

"I need to put on a condom." He reached into his pocket.

"Shhh, my treat I said." Leanne returned to sucking away on her man's hard cock. She hadn't done this in a long time and was relishing turning him on. Quickly, she felt him harden and pulled her mouth away. With her hand on his cock, she reached between his legs and stroked his perineum, before pressing her finger to his anus.

Colin moaned. Leanne pulled away and directed him to the bushes beside them. He sprayed a load of white milky sperm all over the greenery and she kept stroking him until he couldn't come anymore. Gently, she took his sensitive cock head back into her mouth and licked and sucked him clean. "See, even men are sensitive in the anus area. Actually, more so than women I've been told."

She stood up and he kissed her deeply while she zipped his cock back into his pants. "Wow, lady, this has been the best couple days of my life. You are amazing."

"Ahhh, thanks. Just a little experienced, that's all. Now, shall we finish our hike or do you need a moment."

"Give me a moment. What about you, can I get you off?" he said as his legs quivered. "I don't think my feet are ready to move just yet. Now I know why one of my buds always dated older women."

"Hey, we've still got another couple of nights and I intend to make the most of it." She patted his subsiding hardness in his jeans. "Later. You're right, I don't want to get down onto the wet ground. Thought I'd give you a treat for the delicious company you've been."

"Like I said, I'm yours to do with whatever you like. Especially after that incredible episode and I do like your idea of bonus pay."

****

"So what do you propose to do next, my knowledgeable escort?" Leanne watched the waves crashing on the shore as the Blackball ferry from Port Angeles, at the top of the Washington Olympic Peninsula, crossed over to Canadian waters and headed for Victoria. The fresh salt smell of the ocean assailed her nose.

Colin smiled warmly. She'd never been up to Canada, thinking like a lot of Americans, it was mountains, Eskimos, and lots of wilderness. She knew different, the prints and adventures of her parents had told her that. Still, it was exciting to enter another country and experience something besides Americanism.

"So if you want something different and money is no object I suggest we night it in the grandest hotel in Victoria. The Fairmont Empress. It is located at the heart of the inner harbor, very poshy, very British, more so than the British, they say." He held her hand while the wind whipped at them and ocean blusters swept them along.

She could see the large landmass of Vancouver Island approaching.

"My parents took me here a couple of times, and I've been told they have a wonderful spa now, very luxurious. They serve a traditional high formal tea in midafternoon."

"Hmmm, never did formal tea, and a massage, together would be nice. Let's do it." She hugged Colin and kissed him. He had been the most pleasant distraction from her suffering she could have ever asked for. What did he call it? "Shag therapy." And in her case, there was nothing wrong with fucking her brains out to relieve the stress of the last few months. With no commitments thrown in, it had been totally unexpected pleasure.

****

They lay side by side in a full body wrap as each got worked over by the masseuse. Leanne had gotten a mud facial and they'd shared masques as well. After the stress-relieving Swedish rubdown, Leanne smiled, wondering if that was the type or the fact that both women were long-haired blondes. She didn't care. She just wanted to relax and have someone perform wonders on her body. The aromatherapy oils soothed her, and the rose oil and petal rubdown was very romantic. Normally she'd be in the mood for more lovemaking but she simply wanted to enjoy the sedate feeling washing over her.

"I'm glad we did the Hip Honeymooner Package.

Let's go for the tea," she said. "I'm feeling aroused, but it is so nice to just wallow in such a relaxed state. We've got a spa in our suite, where we could have more fun later." The fragrances of rose oil and rosehip lingered in the air and all over her. The two women had brushed them side by side before being massaged. Although Colin looked uncomfortable at first, he soon got into the spirit.

Colin smiled back, as he rose from his table. "Yes, very relaxed. I like the wallowing idea—never had a massage before, delicious."

****

Totally relaxed, Leanne stared out the window of the Empress' Tea Lobby. The room was set exquisitely in posh Victorian style, with wingback chairs, tables of oak and teak, venerable tapestries, and lovely rugs filled the room. She could smell the soothing fragrant oils still soaking into her skin. Colin merely smiled as they sat across from each other, holding hands.

The tea service had arrived with silver platters and delicate china cups. Everything was so upper-class sophisticated. She loved being spoiled and definitely could get used to being a rich cultured woman. "This is an amazing city. If we had more time I'd tour us around, but tonight I'd just like to have supper here after we retire to our room and hopefully no rude Greeks to catch my food."

"I hear they get the orca's to spit some of their catch back."

Leanne laughed. "You really are great company. You said quite a handful of famous people have stayed here. Oh, and I'll say this again. Thanks, Colin, for making this grieving lady get over her past." She nibbled at the fresh scones and delicate pastries. The heady aroma of the dark Ceylon teas stirred her senses back to life from the lethargic state the spa and rubdowns had put her into.

"Leanne, it's me that has to thank you, it has been my utmost pleasure serving you. I'll never forget these few days we've had together. There are even reports of ghost maids wandering the halls. I've read the Queen and many famous movie stars going way back to the thirties have stayed here."

"Wonderful place, glad you suggested it." She felt a light throb at the thought of the Collette ghost in her dreams. "Oh, and it isn't over yet. You want to go up to Tofino? The tourist brochures show Long Beach and some trails with trees that have trunks as big around as this room. I walked around a couple in the Redwoods of California. Makes me feel rather small and humble."

"Not to mention some of the wildest night clubs, lots of younger people hang out there. Lots do surfing on waves, that they say rival Hawaii even. Long beach has sand that stretches for miles."

"You've sold me. Tofino it is and something tells me we may find even more adventure up there." She always trusted her intuition and it was calling her to go there, not sure why, but Leanne knew to go with the flow. It had treated her well and had given her Colin these last couple of days.

"Why are you coming up here to Canada again? Never did tell me. Anything to do with those old CPR prints in your trunk?"

She stared out across the inner harbor, the dome legislature building next to them, probably built around the same time as the hotel added to the feel of age and class. "Yeah, I was just thinking how this room reminded me of those prints. I guess the English had a large part in developing Canada and the railroads that run through the country. My mom met my dad at Lake Louise and she always said it was a magical place, along with Banff. It made her yearn to want to paint. My mom was very talented, but almost never painted. It wasn't encouraged back in her time. After she died, I read her diaries and found out how much she wanted to be an artist. Instead, she raised us kids and looked after my dad. Sad, really.

"So he and my husband died, on the same day, I got the news virtually minutes apart. I decided I wanted these from their house and would come out to visit. I always wanted to paint and hearing Mom's story, I knew now was the time to follow my heart's desire, before it's too late."

Colin brushed her hand. "Lady, you make me want to hold you. I know you'll find that important someone out there. But I think for now, I agree, more shag therapy and go after your dreams."

Leanne giggled, setting down the delicate rose-decorated teacup. "Well now, all those oils and hands relaxing me, have indeed made me want to enjoy you some more. Let's go back to our room and try some Colin therapeutic intervention before I get too melancholy."

She held his arm as they entered the room. "Now, on the bed naked, condom on, and I'm going to show you what a lady on top can do."

They both quickly undressed and Colin lay on the bed, his manhood proudly standing at attention. Yes, she liked having someone this young and ready to make love on a moment's notice.

Leanne got on top and slid herself down over his erection, feeling his hardness filling her as she lowered herself. "Now you just relax and let me do all the work."

"Oh man, lady, it's your dime. I'm just happy to serve."

"You sure you don't have RCMP Mountie blood in you? Actually, I can feel where all of your blood is right now." She moaned as she leaned forward, kissing him, her breasts crushed against his chest. Leanne slowly began to move at leisure on his cock. She sat up, her hands on his shoulders, and closed her eyes, reveling in the feel of hard maleness sliding in her. "Fondle my breasts. Love the feel of hands on them pinching my nipples."

Colin did, his rough hands squeezing the softness between them. His fingers brushed at her nipples still soaking in oils. Very erect and aroused. She had loved the feel of the lady massaging her earlier, and if Colin wasn't with her, she'd have hinted at perhaps a more personal massage. But Leanne knew that these professional massage therapists didn't do that. The fantasy was arousing though. She wondered what that woman's hands would have felt like on her. Perhaps softly reaching between her thighs as she lay there, fondling her swollen pussy lips. Her expert fingers sliding into her wetness as she lay there, relaxed and allowing the woman to masturbate her. Slowly, so slowly as she lay in the moist air, filled with sensual oils and fragrances.

Leanne could still smell the exotic fragrances of the oils washing over her as the heat of her body released the vapors. She felt bad she really should be thinking of Colin and his hardness rubbing against her G-spot. All she could concentrate on was that woman's hands all over her body. Working their magic.

She felt herself beginning to build as she fantasized about the earlier encounter. Was it that she desired a woman as much as a man lately? Or more?

The dream earlier on the holiday with Colette—so erotic. To be taken by her, helpless, as she mounted her.

Leanne gasped as her internal flood exploded, like a tsunami washing all the stress from her.

"God, you were amazing," she lied as she collapsed to his body.

"I didn't really do anything." He stared, puzzled at her as he kissed her.

"Just fuck me silly now." Leanne moaned as he moved her off him and got on top. Leanne grabbed the headboard behind her as he began to thrust away. Nothing wrong with a hard, willing man, she thought. Also nothing wrong with a soft, slow caress of a woman as well. That was it—she'd have to find a woman for their threesome, but was it more for him or for herself?

Chapter Four

They'd driven up Vancouver Island to Nanaimo and inland toward Tofino, stopping only at the Cathedral grove in MacMillan park just outside of Port Alberni. Leanne couldn't believe the size of the old trees, some as big as eight people across and one where several trunks had grown together, forming a massive dense structure.

The wilds of Canada were totally amazing and beyond anything she'd been exposed to anywhere in America. they caught pictures of elk and even black bears ambling along the side of the road. She could only wonder what the Canadian Rockies were like, and not surprised that her mom so loved the area.

He took her hand as they reached the Tofino headland and led her onto the natural beach of Long Beach. Miles and miles of just them and sand, with the ocean crashing at low tide. Leanne spent half the day just strolling the shore, picking up seashells and watching crabs scuttle in tiny ponds as they waited for the water to return to wash them home again.

She picked the nicest looking hotel to retire to right off the beach, Wickaninnish Inn, just off Chesterman Beach, where the natives had a carving shed and an Ancient Cedars spa. Leanne smiled to herself. if they didn't find a woman tonight, she might have to visit the spa and hope for the best. After all, if she could seduce such a virile young man like Colin, who knew, maybe a Colinette would do as well. She smiled as they checked in. Perhaps she had time for another round before they went out.

****

She trusted Colin's judgement and let him take them to the Wild Shelters bar in town. It hung on the second level of a restaurant, supported by ancient cedar beams, but tonight wasn't about the view outside. It was about dancing and feeling the rhythm of the music thumping away, and as Leanne caught a lady about Colin's age watching them from her seat, perhaps finding a woman for both of them to enjoy. She wasn't sure if the girl was watching her or Colin or both. The techno music pounded in the background, and lights and strobe balls flashed as Leanne occasionally glanced at her. The woman stared intensely at the two of them.

The young woman was in a crowd of younger ladies, perhaps a hen night or just the girls getting out. She had long wavy blonde hair, her blouse, like a lot of the younger ladies, was opened and her very full breasts nearly spilled out. The rest of her filled the curves of her tight jeans. She reminded her of a younger Sam, who had seduced her in her lingerie store.

Leanne slid herself over Colin's leg, doing a slow sensual dirty dog routine, and turned him around so that his back was to the bar. The woman's eyes were definitely glued on the two of them as she casually talked with her friends. She smiled at the girl and Leanne caught a hint of a smile and a shy smirk back. The young lady's hand was resting between her jean-covered thighs. Was she covertly playing with herself, fantasizing? Maybe she wasn't just staring at Colin?

Leanne nudged Colin back to their table. "We need to talk."

They sat down to order another round of drinks as the song ended. The girl's gaze seemed to follow them. Leanne leaned into Colin, yelling in his ear as the music began to pound away again. "What do you think? Does that luscious-looking blonde look tasty enough to join us tonight? The one over by the bar, lots of curls and curves, with the purple top, kinda looks like some pro-sports cheerleader."

Colin glanced at her. "Are you kidding me? She's an absolute knockout. Surely she's here with some hunky guy; can't be alone."

"She's not alone, with a group of other ladies. But she's been watching us, a lot, and when I winked at her, she smiled back."

Colin's eyes widened. "You don't think?"

"I think. She's interested, just not sure who. Before some guy makes his move, I'm going over to talk to her while you sip your drink. So stay here, I'm going to introduce myself and see. I think she'd be very yummy in our bed tonight." Leanne looked up, the curvy blonde was still sitting there quietly, her group of friends had, for the most part, got up and were dancing in a group around their purses. She was still stealing looks Leanne's way. Leanne smiled at her again. The lady blinked and shyly looked at her drink instead. She was watching them, all right, and Leanne was sure it was more like watching her.

"Oh God, if I'm allowed to say this in your company. I'm already getting stiff just visualizing you and her."

"Well save some of that wetness for later, if she

joins us, it'll be a hot night, I think. What I realized a long time ago, most very gorgeous women, like her, are often very lonely. Few guys have the guts to approach her, at least not before they have several drinks under their belts. Wish me luck, 'cause I'm getting wet myself." She kissed Colin on the cheek.

"You're right about that. I wouldn't have the guts to approach her, drinks or no drinks." He stared at her and the lady, smiling.

She already knew what kind of lascivious thoughts were steamrolling through his mind. The same as hers.

Not believing she would have the guts to pull this off, Leanne walked up to the lady. As Janice once said when they were in the middle of abducting a famous actress as part of her husband's fantasy and realized that the lady had no idea what was going on, *'It's either we play this for real or we possibly end up in jail.'*

So, she decided to lay it on thick. "Hi, I'm Leanne and I couldn't help but notice that you had your eye on my partner and I while we were dancing."

She smiled innocently at Leanne as she sipped her drink. Leanne looked her up and down, her eyes falling into the deep cleavage she wanted to run her tongue over. "Or is it more that you've got your eye on me?" The last sentence she leaned in and whispered loudly in her ear. Her breath hot.

The girl shuddered and stared virtually straight into the cleavage of Leanne's breasts from where she sat on the bar stool. She licked her lips as Leanne straightened up. There was no doubt that this girl wanted her. "I...I..."

This was the moment to go over the top. "Honey, don't be ashamed to say it. If I wasn't with Colin there, who's a pretty fine-looking young stud if I say so myself, I'd be asking you to dance and taking you up to my hotel room for more than a nightcap." She brushed her hand slowly along the young lady's arm.

The curvy blonde smiled at her. Leanne could see lust building in her eyes like a thunderstorm rolling off the coast. This woman wanted her. "Amanda." Her voice was quiet as she spoke to Leanne, trembling as Leanne continued to run her fingers along the woman's arm. She felt the shivers ranging through the younger lady. "It's just that my former gym teacher was a redhead and looked a lot like you and..."

She fell silent.

Leanne grinned at her, she already knew the answer curving through the sub-conscious lust of this woman. She leaned in again and whispered against her ear, her hot breath washing into the woman. "Let me guess, she seduced you into girl-on-girl action and as much as you want to deny it, you really enjoyed it." Leanne let her hand rest on the lady's thigh as she spoke, her fingers slightly squeezing the soft flesh. The woman involuntarily parted them slightly and even though she'd barely been off the bar stool, Leanne felt the heat through her jeans.

Amanda moaned as Leanne leaned in again and licked quickly at her ear. "Don't be shy, tell me the truth."

"Yes." A deep husky response came back.

"And you want me. Want me to take you." She'd read this woman perfectly.

"Yes." A deeper, quieter second response.

Oh, it's going to be one delicious night. Hope we can find a way to get Colin involved, cause this woman is going to be all mine. "Let me buy you a drink. We can dance a bit and get to know each other. Colin could join us later. We could make it a hot threesome in our hotel room."

Her eyes widened as she looked at Colin. The woman was probably bi, definitely not straight though. Leanne ran her hand up her inside thigh slightly and squeezed again. She sighed, and the intensity increased in her blue eyes. The woman was most definitely in heat for another woman to take her. "He'd be okay with that? What if I want to spend most of the night with you?"

The first obvious sign she was more than willing to have sex with Leanne. "I'm sure he'll be okay with anything you want to do. I think he virtually popped his load at the mention that I wanted you in my bed tonight, more for me than him." She ran her hand up the lady's arm. She could see the goosebumps erupting down her arm. Leanne was certain she'd have to lead tonight. This woman was very open to being seduced by her. In fact, she already was, the rest was up to Leanne.

Amanda stared at Leanne as she caressed her arm. *Kiss me here and now* was written all over the desires racing through her widening eyes. "White wine with a twist of lemon."

As all the stools were full, Leanne stood next to the gorgeous full-bodied blonde. Her tight jeans straining to keep those lovely full thighs in place. Leanne whispered to her as she caught Colin staring anxiously at them. "You've such wonderful waves in your hair. Are these natural?" she asked and ran one hand through Amanda's flowing tresses. She purposely ran her hand down the side of her neck, caressing her skin. The lady moaned. "Oh yes, all natural."

She reached up and placed a hand around Leanne, resting it just about the top of her rear. She rubbed her hand back and forth.

"Start touching me any lower and I won't be waiting for our man to join us," Leanne whispered in her ear and played the game she was sure this woman was into. "I usually like my women more submissive."

Amanda boldly slid her hand slightly lower and pinched one of Leanne's cheeks through her dress. "As soon as our drinks arrive, I want to feel you next to me on the dance floor," she whispered into Leanne's ear, her breath hot with desire.

Leanne leaned into her and kissed her quickly on the lips. "So do I since I have a thing for delicious curvy blondes." She heard the girl gasp.

By now Colin was probably stroking himself in his jeans. The night had suddenly turned out to be a welcome surprise as most of this trip had been, and she knew whatever they did, Colin would never forget it. Hell, she probably wouldn't either.

When the drinks arrived, they both took deep gulps. Leanne maintaining control, grabbed her by the hand, and pulled her onto the dance floor, eager to be on the dance floor, touching each other. She put her arm around the nubile blonde and put one leg between her thighs as they danced close. She could feel the heat from her center against her thigh. Amanda moaned, obviously like Leanne it was a real thrill to be taken by another woman—someone stronger and in charge, only it was Leanne doing the leading this time.

They gyrated together for a while to one song. Leanne planted several kisses on her neck. The lady returned it by sucking on hers. Their breasts crushed together. All the time the blonde was rubbing herself on Leanne's thigh. She obviously liked the sensation of being masturbated or, as some women liked, tribbing together. Something she hadn't tried, but the thought suddenly seemed very delicious.

"Let's get him up before he blows his load and feels left out," Leanne said into Amanda's ear. She waved him up to join them. "Colin, Amanda. Amanda, Colin. As you can see, Amanda and I have gotten very acquainted, and she said she'd love to join us for a hot threesome after some dancing to work us up."

She could see Colin's cock bulging against the material of his jeans. Amanda glanced at it, at him, and back to Leanne. "Yes, I would," was all she could muster as Colin put his arms around the two. He stood behind Amanda as Leanne stood in front of her. The music and lights pounded away.

"Ah, an Amanda sandwich. Such a tasty morsel, don't you think?"

Colin rubbed himself against Amanda's very round ass. "Oh yes, most scrumptious." He kissed Leanne as the three pressed against each other, his hands running up and down her sides. His eyes widened with desire and thanks. They alternated the rest of the night, dancing with eventually each of them in the center. The music pounded, and they performed more sexual posing than dancing with each other. Colin was in heaven at one point as Amanda danced in front of him and pretended to go to her knees, while Leanne rubbed the sides of his thighs.

Laughing, they rushed from the bar and staggered down the sidewalk to the inn, just a block over,

Amanda holding onto Leanne. At one point, Leanne leaned into her and gave her a deep French kiss, then Colin frenched her. "I take it you want to be the focus of our sexual desires tonight?" Leanne asked.

"Yes, I'm so turned on." Leanne kissed her deeply again as Colin's eyes bulged.

"It is so hot to watch two women necking. The inn is this way."

The three fell into the hotel room. Leanne knew she'd have to keep up the pretense of being in charge. At least she knew Amanda was totally turned on by having a redhead control her, perhaps living out some fantasy from her past with the first woman who seduced her to the dark side. Leanne smirked to herself. "Colin, put on the music, something nice and slow. Be a dear and pour us some wine. I think you might like to watch Amanda and me dance and neck together. I know I want to dance with her." Colin turned on the TV and tuned into an all-music channel that had mellow romantic tunes.

Leanne wondered if she was insane to do this, even though she was having the time of her life. "Now come here, you delicious looking blonde." She spun Amanda around and pulled her into her arms. Their breasts crushed together. Excitement smoked from the lady's eyes. She definitely thrilled to the domination of another woman. Leanne knew what that was like. Being helpless while a stronger female took advantage of her. The thrill of living some dark fantasy against one's will, but wanting it to happen regardless of how perverse or taboo the thought was.

Amanda collapsed into her arms. Her arms went around Leanne's neck and Leanne bent her mouth to the offered red lipstick lips. They kissed deeply, Amanda allowing Leanne's probing tongue to enter her mouth. She sucked on it a moment before they continued kissing, then thrusting her crotch against Leanne. A guttural moan escaped both their lips. She was doing everything to arouse Leanne and it was working. Virtually flinging herself at the mature redhead.

To hell with the dancing. Leanne pulled the blonde's shirt free of her jeans with one hand and reached up over the hot soft skin of the lady's back. A flick and the bra was undone. She reached up and began to fondle the overly full breasts that were barely contained under, what she guessed were a 38 D cup. Nipples tightened at her touch. Amanda sucked at her tongue. She wanted this very badly. "Oh God, I want to please you, any way you would like me to." She gasped as Leanne pinched her nipples.

Her words set a signal in Leanne's mind. "Good, nothing like a submission. I think we should show Colin how much, like maybe I should make you get on your knees pleasuring me with your tongue."

Amanda shuddered at the thought and kissed Leanne back. "Please, make me." A low grunt of need escaped her lips. This woman was hers to use as she pleased tonight. "And I want to suck on these nipples. God, you've got large, soft breasts."

The song ended, and Leanne kissed her deeply again. "First, I need to use the washroom and get a drink of wine. I think Colin might feel more than a little left out. As they say in the world of team wrestling, tag you're it, Colin. I think I've got her worked up enough."

Before she came back into the room, Leanne peeled off her blouse and shed her skirt. Dressed only in lavender bra and panties, she entered the room to find Amanda on Colin's lap, necking with him. He had her top unbuttoned, bra lifted, and was fondling her large exposed breasts.

Colin stopped as Leanne entered the room. Amanda stared at Leanne, licking her lips. She was more into wanting Leanne than Colin right now. She whispered into his ear, "Yes, go for it. I'll get mine later."

He smirked at Leanne. "Oh really, I'd rather watch you two, myself." He grinned.

"Well, that's easily arranged, your wish is my desire." She pecked him on the cheek and looked at Amanda. "Now, I thought you were more into me than a man. I want you to beg for it. So first of all, I want you to get on your knees and come to me on all fours. I've a hunch you like to be dominated, don't you? Say it." Leanne spoke as she strolled across the room.

"Yes." She dropped to her knees as Leanne walked across the room. Colin's eyes nearly popped out of his head.

"Yes, what?" Leanne spoke sharply.

"Yes, Mistress." The young blonde slowly crawled on all fours to Leanne

Colin watched, his cock jumping in his pants. Her gym teacher had obviously dominated her in the past, that and possibly more.

Amanda looked up at her. "I'm very okay with letting you have me any way you want. I'm yours in servitude. I can't help it, I wanted to be naked in your arms the moment I saw the two of you on the dance floor."

Leanne smiled at her. "I know."

Colin leaned back in his chair, sipping on his wine. "Don't let me interrupt you ladies. I've always wanted to watch two women make love to each other. I might not be able to help myself and might even have to stroke myself for relief."

Leanne smiled at him and then Amanda as the blonde slowly approached her. "Anytime you want to join in you can. I think I'm going to make her my lesbian love slave tonight. I've a hunch you've been dominated before. Haven't you?"

"Yes, Mistress," she said looking at Leanne softly.

"After I have fun using my little slave here, be my guest, Colin, she'll be all yours. First, stand and take all of your clothes off. I want to see the woman I'm going to make love to naked."

Amanda did, slowly taking off the rest of her clothes. Her gaze never left Leanne's as she stripped. Leanne nearly whistled at the woman's figure—in calling her a cheerleader she wasn't far off. Amanda looked shyly down, obviously embarrassed. "Do I look okay?"

"Okay?" Colin sputtered. "You'd beat out most Playboy pinup centerfold girls." His eyes drank in her figure.

Tan lines accented her heavy full un-tanned breasts. Leanne always found that quite attractive in women. She had a very soft curve to her hips and full round ass cheeks, again un-tanned. She, like most of the younger generation, had shaved her dark triangle and only left a small strip behind. Her stomach was tight and a small diamond hung from her navel.

"Nice, very nice. Now on your knees again as you approach your mistress. Because that's what you've wanted to do all night, isn't it? Please me with your mouth."

She sank to her knees and quietly said, "Yes, Mistress."

"I'll bet that's what your teacher made you do, isn't it? Give her pleasure. I'll bet she made you satisfy her, didn't she? Maybe even spank you first. Make you beg to pleasure her."

"Yes. How did you know?"

"I know because I've been you. Hungry to pleasure another woman. Tell me about the first time."

Amanda stared, obviously a little stunned. Leanne had just read the truth of what had happened to her. "She spanked me, only I got very aroused and she knew. Next, she pulled down my panties, fondled me, and over her knees masturbated me to an orgasm." Amanda stopped, her face turning red, embarrassed to continue in front of strangers.

"Tell me what you had to do next." She already knew, she just wanted to hear it from her lips, for Colin's benefit.

"I had to pleasure her with my mouth," Amanda admitted as she sat on her haunches before Leanne. Her face only inches from Leanne's pussy.

Leanne knew from the night with Sam and Janice how sexually arousing it was to be spanked naked over another woman's knees and have to pleasure her after. "Spread your thighs and reach between your legs, my submissive lover. Slide that finger between your wetness and let me see if you're wet enough." Amanda did and offered her finger to Leanne.

Leanne leaned over and sucked slowly on the wet fingers like she had on Colin's cock the day before. "Yes, I think you are very wet and want me, aren't you?"

"Yes, Mistress." She bowed her head in submission. Colin had unzipped his pants and was stroking himself. His eyes were on the tableau unfolding before his unbelieving, thankful eyes.

"I do believe you are ready to pleasure your mistress. Take my panties off, now."

Amanda reached up, her manicured hands shaking, and slowly pulled down Leanne's lavender panties. It was quite the thrill to have this incredibly sexy woman craving to have sex with her. To do anything Leanne wanted. Unlike the younger crowd, Leanne preferred to keep a fuller bush and just trimmed it lower along her lips. No sense in having tall grass in the playground someone once told her.

"Like it, my dear?"

"Yes, Mistress. Very full, dark and…dominating."

Leanne placed a finger between her labia lips and offered it to the lust-ridden blonde. "Taste me first."

Amanda very slowly and tenderly licked at Leanne's finger with the softest of kisses. Her hot wanting mouth sucked at Leanne's moist finger as she moaned deep in her throat. Oh yes, she had definitely liked being another woman's submissive lover. "Now put your nose to my pussy and breathe deep. I want you to show Colin how hungry you've made me for your tongue and lips."

"Please, Mistress. Please, let me satisfy you." Leanne looked up, the hunger in her eyes betraying her. Colin's eyes were focused on the two of them, slowly stroking his hard-on. Even if he came now, she knew he'd be able to go again, and it didn't look like he'd last for much longer.

"You may pleasure your mistress now and don't stop until you've made me come."

Amanda's tongue flicked out as she dove into Leanne's wet pussy lips. Slowly, she ran her tongue along the vee of Leanne's labia. A low moan escaped her lips as she licked Leanne and occasionally sucked softly on the exposed bud of her clit. She'd done this many times to her last female lover, Leanne knew. Very well trained. "Now, show Colin how much you enjoy licking your mistress. Let him watch you masturbate. I want you to come with your mouth on me. Hungry to eat another woman's pussy."

Amanda did, her fingers rubbing herself between the legs. Colin watched mesmerized as she submitted herself fully. Leanne reached down and held her head, grinding her face with her pussy. She could tell by the girl's loud moans she was already beginning to come, lost in her internal ecstasy. Amanda gasped into Leanne's wetness, her body convulsing as her orgasm exploded through her. Her mouth sucking on her pussy hungrily. "Don't stop until I come…suck my clit." Amanda did, her convulsions continuing to rip through her. Perhaps this was the lady's darkest fantasy, to admit to wanting to be a slave to another woman's pussy while a man watched her. Leanne had a new appreciation for voyeurs. Colin was stroking himself quicker now—how he hadn't released his load yet she had no idea. "Put your hands on my ass and hold my pussy to your mouth."

Amanda did and continued drowning herself in the

wetness of Leanne's pussy as she kept rubbing herself on her wanting mouth. Leanne could feel herself erupting on the girl's mouth. "Stick your fingers into me now."

She shrieked as Amanda did, and flung her wet lips hard against the wanting woman as she exploded. Shuddering, she looked up and watched as Colin had stopped stroking himself, probably too close to the edge of coming.

"Enough, my slave." She shook as she pulled Amanda away from her pussy. "Now I think you've over-aroused Colin and he wants to join us." Leanne unfastened her bra. "I expect those lips to continue to suck my pussy as I do the same to yours. I'll lie on the bed and you get over me."

"Thank you." Amanda rose and Leanne kissed her full on the lips, licking her juices off her. "Thank you," she repeated.

"You'll thank me even more later. Now, I think this is just the beginning of a long night of lovemaking, don't you?"

Softly, she said, "Yes, my Mistress." Leanne slapped the woman hard on the ass as she turned to get on the bed. Amanda gave a sharp shriek. The jiggle of her bottom very sexy. "Hmmm, I might have to redden those cheeks later."

"If it pleases you, my Mistress. I am yours to do with as you like."

"I know, that is very exciting to have my own willing lesbian slave." Leanne laid herself out on the bed. "Now bring me that wonderfully looking swollen pussy. I want to lick you awhile before Colin is ready to take you for himself."

Colin nodded as he sipped on his wine and reached for a condom. His cock was hard and throbbing—it wouldn't take him long to erupt—and probably why he stopped earlier.

Leanne lay on the bed and Amanda eagerly got on top. She lowered her pussy to Leanne's waiting mouth. Her hot mouth returned to licking and sucking on Leanne's pussy as Leanne ran her tongue along the lady's wet slit. She heard the woman moan and buck slightly as Leanne began to flick her tongue through the very wet groove. She knew Amanda was near to another orgasm.

Leanne felt the bed shift. She stopped a moment. Colin mounted himself above the two women, behind Amanda's raised ass. "Slide into Amanda's wet pussy while I continue to eat her out. It won't take long for her to come again or you for that matter."

He did, and they both moaned as Leanne felt the girl begin to spasm, lost in a world of intense pleasure. He thrust hard into her as she screamed her release into Leanne's pussy.

"Oh fuck, don't stop."

The lady went off the deep end, spasming as Colin grabbed her by the hips and kept plunging hard and fast inside her. Leanne clamped her lips onto her clit and sucked lightly.

She could feel Colin approaching his own orgasm—how he had kept himself back so far was beyond her. Leanne reached up and played with his testicles before sliding her finger along the groove between his cheeks. He clenched himself and quickly shot his load as he thrust forward hard. Leanne continued licking at the writhing Amanda.

Amanda collapsed in a mess. Colin kissed Amanda on the back, cupping her breasts, and got off the bed, his legs shaking. "I'll be back for more in a moment. Gotta remove this and take a pee. That was amazing." He leaned over and kissed Leanne before trudging off to the washroom. His eyes squinted in thanks. She surmised that in his wildest dreams, he probably never expected this tonight.

Amanda rolled off Leanne. "Oh, this is so hot. I love it, Mistress." Leanne turned around and frenched the hot blonde. Her hand fondled the curvy ass cheeks. Amanda leaned into her, threading her arms around Leanne. Her breasts crushing against her.

"The feeling of your hands on my rear is wonderful." Leanne looked down at her. "Well, now that's a thought. My hands adorning your rear-end. I think it's time I gave you a good spanking."

"Please, Mistress, I've been such a bad girl today. Please don't spank me." The woman was begging for it. She had to ask her later more about her past. There was something so intensely erotic about being a submissive woman to another female.

Colin returned and sat back watching the two women kissing and Leanne fondling her ass.

He sipped at his wine.

Leanne broke their embrace to get up and sit on the other padded chair in the room. She sipped her wine for a moment. "Stand up, Amanda, and put your hands behind you." Amanda scrambled out of bed eagerly. *Oh yeah, she definitely wants this.* Leanne remembered the scene where she was naked over Sam's legs being spanked and Janice finished her off, licking her from behind. "Turn around." God, she had an incredibly hot body. "I think that wonderful ass needs some color added to it. Don't you, Colin?"

"Well, that's something I haven't seen before. Sounds very erotic."

"Don't you agree, my submissive lover?" Leanne wanted the lady to beg for it.

"Yes, Mistress, I'd love for you to spank me. I deserve it."

Leanne patted her thighs. "Over my legs, now."

Amanda lowered herself over Leanne's knees. Leanne reached around and, as Colin watched, she pinched those nipples, hard with want.

He watched intently at the wobble of Amanda's cheeks as Leanne smacked the woman's rear a couple of times. Her cheeks jiggled at the sharp cracks that rang in the air. She rubbed them, slipping her hand between her legs. Amanda moaned loudly. "Colin, give me a minute to get her ready for you. Can you go another round?"

"Oh yeah, this is such a kinky turn-on."

She could see his cock stirring already.

"Now, my bad girl, prepare yourself." Leanne swatted her harder, first on one cheek, then the other. Amanda groaned, very aroused as Leanne played with her nipples.

Leanne reached between the woman's legs and slid her finger down the wet slit of her pussy. Amanda widened her stance, eagerly responding to Leanne's actions with an obvious voracious hunger. She'd done this before, of that there was no doubt, enjoying having another woman masturbate her.

Leanne spread her cheeks apart slightly. "Ever let a man take you here?" she said, licking one of her fingers and running it along the brown wrinkled entrance to her anus before slipping it inside. Amanda moaned loudly.

"No, Mistress." She groaned, obviously excited at the thought of a man taking her ass.

"Well, your master over there is very willing to break you in and masters like to take their slaves up the ass. Don't they, Colin?"

He nodded, stiff at the thought.

"But first, I think you need some lubrication. Colin, get behind her and lube up this sexy entrance," she said gruffly.

Colin quickly got behind Amanda and slowly licked the woman's wrinkled anal entrance. She moaned loudly. Leanne slipped a hand under her to finger her clit. "Don't forget to lick her pussy as well. I think she has plenty of lube for you to find there." The woman was bucking as Colin licked, stabbing his hard tongue first into one hole and then the other. "After all, a good servant must satisfy any needs of their master and mistress. Don't you agree, my blonde submissive?"

"Yes, Mistress, I must do whatever is asked of me to satisfy my masters." Leanne smacked her ass a few more times, now glowing a wonderful blush red color.

"Now get a rubber after our bad girl lubes your cock with her mouth."

Colin moved around to Amanda's mouth. "Suck him well or you'll get more of this." Leanne swatted her ass a few times as Amanda opened her lips and let Colin slide his throbbing cock down her throat. Leanne stroked her between the legs as the gorgeous blonde ran her tongue on the underside of his cock, lapping up his length as he slid into her wanting throat.

"This is amazing—she's amazing." Colin gasped

as Amanda sucked on his hardness. He slid himself in and out of her eager mouth, listening to her panting.

"Now, my dear, your master will take the last of your holes for his pleasure."

She spread Amanda's cheeks apart and guided Colin's cock to her entrance. "Slow and easy. Let her get used to having your cock inside."

He fought a little to get past the sphincter ring as Leanne continued to finger the groaning girl, helping her to relax. Colin slowly slid his cock into her, working his way back and forth, going deeper each time. "Fuck, she's so tight."

"This is so dirty and sexy." Amanda moaned. "No one has ever done this to me before. I feel so taken."

"Yes, you are. Helpless to be taken, however it pleases us tonight. Understood?" Leanne slapped one of her ass cheeks, rubbing in the domination angle. Colin moaned as Amanda clenched. "This is what happens to you when you don't behave. Now fuck her gorgeous ass nice and slow, while I finger our lovely entertainment for the night."

Colin slid himself back and forth. Amanda began to buck, obviously liking her first anal fucking as Colin increased his pace. "I'm coming already."

Leanne could see her flexing her muscles and Colin groaning in response. She smacked her ass cheeks as she reached around and rubbed the woman's throbbing clit. Amanda cried out as she began to come. Leanne leaned over and kissed Colin. With his hands on her hips, he thrust harder.

"Oh," was all that came out of his lips as he slammed into her. Amanda didn't seem to mind and kept groaning, bucking herself against Leanne's hand, enjoying the threesome.

Colin fell over the prone lady, gasping for air. His hands positioned around Amanda's midsection. "That was incredibly wild, so tight." He gasped as he pulled out and stood up to kiss Leanne. The biggest satisfied grin crossed his face as his eyes cried 'thank you' to her. Leanne winked back.

"I guess I've got to go clean myself off again." He smirked as he walked to the washroom, legs shaking. "This is getting to be a regular habit."

Leanne sighed. "Oh, I hope you've got a good supply of condoms, and the willingness to keep going."

"Give me a minute, another glass of wine and your lips. I'll be going for a hat-trick. That was such an erotic fantasy come true."

Amanda sank to her knees in front of Leanne. "Such a turn-on, doesn't even begin to sum it up. Never knew anything that rude could be so sexy. Letting a man take my ass. Thank you, Mistress." She kissed Leanne's thighs, rubbed her bottom before putting her hand on Leanne's legs. She tenderly kissed Leanne's thigh, her tongue licking at her flesh. Obviously, the lady wasn't done yet, which was good, neither was Leanne.

"For some, being dominated and taken is a large turn-on. So I think it is highly unfair that you two get off and I don't. Now, my submissive, use that tongue again on my toes." She lifted her leg and Amanda immediately began to lick and suck on her toes. "I think my little slave girl is far from being satisfied yet, isn't she?"

"Yes, Mistress." She licked and sucked on the offered toes like some delicious cock.

Colin returned, grabbed his glass of wine, and watched with interest as he sat back on the edge of the bed. Leanne watched as he stared at Amanda, a slight smile and a soft look crossed his face. Was it possible he was beginning to fall for the luscious blonde?

"So, my still horny submissive one, I think it is most unfair, while our master rests, that you have all of your orifices serviced and leave your mistress lacking, don't you?"

"Yes, Mistress." Her lips glistened with moisture from sucking on Leanne's toes. "Most unfair, I must make amends."

This woman definitely liked having a woman in control. Leanne leaned over and kissed her deeply, Amanda sucking on her tongue. And she had to admit, just a little part of her really enjoyed being in control and dominating this hungry-to-serve woman. "Now, I'm going to turn around and lean against this chair. You better make good use of that wonderful tongue on my ass and lick me good while I play with myself."

Amanda's eyes opened in pleasure. "Yes, Mistress."

Leanne spread her legs and leaned far over the back of the chair. With one hand, she slipped between her pussy lips and began to finger herself. Amanda kissed each cheek passionately. She ran her tongue along the redhead's crack and down to her anus. Her mouth and tongue began to apply themselves hungrily. "I think our sub has done this before, don't you?"

Colin watched with great focus. "Either that or she's just discovered she finds the sudden idea of doing things anal quite stimulating. Which sounds great to me."

Leanne looked up into the room's mirror and watched as Amanda, on her knees, continued to stroke her tongue on her ass. "Stick your tongue in, fuck me as I come." She did.

Leanne began to finger herself faster, the sight of this most luscious woman before her such a turn-on. She came all too fast.

Leanne slumped into the chair as she exploded. Amanda ran her tongue up her back and kissed the back of her neck. "I hope I've given my mistress a much-needed release?"

"Oh yes. I think it's my turn to get some wine and rest. But I see you have aroused our man again." They both glanced at Colin, his cock hard.

"What can I say? Watching two gorgeous women making love is a massive turn-on. Come here, Amanda."

"She's all yours. I think I could be done for the night." Leanne turned herself around and flopped into the padded chair. Fatigue strained at her limbs as she stroked herself to the subsiding shudders. "Too damn good, I think he's right. You two have some fun together."

Amanda crawled onto the bed, and lying beside Colin, kissed him passionately. Her hand went to his cock and began to stroke him. "Is the master ready to take me again?" She groaned, obviously wanting more.

The insatiability of youth, Leanne thought. A few years ago she might have gotten back on the bed with them. The oak and grape of the wine sank into her throat. It was enough to just sit and watch.

Colin ran his hands over her breasts, fondling and pinching her nipples. "Feed them to me," he said as he leaned back. She got on top and lifted her breasts to his lips where he began to suck and lick at her nipples, crowned with a darker, large area of aureole. First one and then the other. Amanda reached back and stroked his now very hard cock.

"Does the master want to take my ass again?" She panted as her hand stroked him.

"First of all, I'd love to do that. But no, I actually want to make love to you normally." He reached for a rubber on the night table.

"Really?" Amanda took it from his hand. "Let me," she said. She ran her hand along his chest softly.

Leanne smiled to herself. *I think these two are made for each other and they don't even know it.*

Colin laid back as the curvy blonde's mouth sank down the length of his cock. "Is it okay if I lubricate you first?" After a minute of pleasuring him, she applied the rubber to his cock.

"Oh yeah." He grabbed her and pushed her on her back. Amanda spread her legs, allowing him between. Colin slid his cock into her and leaned forward to kiss her. Amanda wrapped her legs around him, obviously enjoying his penetration. They kissed as he slowly thrust into her.

Leanne watched. They looked more like they were making love and not outright fucking. He muttered her name as he thrust into her. Amanda did the same, licking at his ear. "Don't stop."

She smirked. *Maybe they'll get together after this and become a couple.* She could see the sparks flying now between the two, each lost in the flesh of the other. Colin came, thrusting hard. Amanda moaned like she was arriving at her orgasm nearly at the same time.

He lay on top of her after, unable to move. Amanda put her arms around him, caressing his hair. Colin lifted his head and softly kissed her. Neither wanted to break their embrace.

Yup, maybe she started something beautiful here. Leanne got up and went to the washroom. When she got back, they'd crawled under the covers. Amanda had her head on top of his chest, and his arm was around her.

She crawled into bed on the other side of Amanda and turned off the lights. "I think this is the end of a wonderful night." The other two simply nodded, sleep already claiming consciousness. She put her hand on Colin's chest and wrapped her fingers into Amanda's.

****

In the morning, sunlight streaming in, Leanne got up and staggered into the washroom. She turned on the shower and stepped into the heavenly feel of warm water cascading down over her. The other two were still out of it after she'd finished.

She opened the shades even more and stared out into the ocean as the morning sun cut the dark sky. Mist, like most mornings, hovered, covering the watery expanse before her. It would usually lift around noon and she'd be able to see for miles, but not all the way to Japan, half a world away as that ghost from the hotel, Tom once told her.

A rustle broke her concentration. Amanda, already well snuggled in his arms, moved closer to Colin. He half-opened his eyes and was running his hand over Amanda's hair. Stroking her. She ran her hand over his chest and smiled as she tried to get even closer to him. They looked so natural and comfortable with each other.

Colin looked Leanne's way and smiled. "Thanks," he muttered to her as he kissed the top of Amanda's head.

Leanne smirked. "My utmost pleasure." She hushed back as she approached the bed trying to find her clothes in the pile thrown aside last night.

Amanda rubbed herself against Colin, looked up at him, and gave him a tender kiss on the lips. "You and Leanne were the most unbelievable thing I've ever experienced." She kissed Colin again, feeling the coarse hairs of his chest. Obviously safe and warm in the comfort of his arms.

Leanne picked through the pile of discarded clothes and began to dress. "Well, hate to say this, but we've got about an hour before check out and I for one am starving. Do you want to join us for breakfast, Amanda?"

"I'd love to, but can I have a shower first?"

"Sure, I've had mine."

She stared up at Colin. "Care to join me?"

His eyes went to her and Leanne. Leanne nodded for him to go for it. Oh, the instant arousal of youth. She'd had enough sex for a few days—hell, the rest of the trip for that matter, but they would probably be at it like rabbits in the shower. "Love to." He kissed her softly.

"Are you sure you're okay with us together? I don't want to offend you, Leanne."

"What, and get another spanking? That was last night, and if I start something like that, we'll never check out of this place."

Amanda scampered into the shower, her wonderful

full ass jiggling. "Come on then, handsome."

Colin rose and followed, glancing again at Leanne. "You sure?"

She laughed, smirking. "Hey, you'd be crazy not to. Don't worry about me. I'm a big girl and besides, I couldn't come again if I wanted to."

Colin disappeared into the washroom. She could hear the two of them giggling, soaping each other and, in the space of a few minutes, Amanda moaning. The shapes behind the curtain in the mirror revealed Colin pinning Amanda up against the wall and slowly fucking her as the waters cascaded down them.

"Oh to be young, foolish, and full of juice. And enough horny energy to do it every minute of the day."

Well, this holiday had taken a most unexpected turn again. She wasn't sure if she was up for any more surprises or crazy nights of rampant sex. Leanne stretched her sore legs as she heard Colin grunt in the shower. The wonderful soreness between her thighs responded to the partial sight of the two of them making love.

I think this time discretion is the better part of valor. She thought as she dressed. *Didn't think I'd have to rest my lady garden on this holiday.*

Amanda moaned again from the showers. "Yup, a couple of years ago, I'd be joining them." She groaned, leaning over to find her handbag, looking for her makeup. Still, it was quite the enjoyable night.

****

The three sat around the breakfast table sipping at their coffees. Subdued mellowness after a night on the town, Leanne smirked. A line she'd read somewhere. "So, Amanda, we could drive you back to wherever you need to get to or you could hang out with us before I make the drive to Nanaimo to catch the ferry for Vancouver?"

She smiled. "How funny. I was going back to Vancouver tonight as well. My girlfriends were going to pick me up. I'd love to hang out with you two if that's okay."

"Sure," Leanne said as Colin looked at her. "Text them and let them know we'll take you into Vancouver tonight. Only, of course, if you're okay with Amanda sitting on your lap, Colin. Could get a little uncomfortable for a couple of hours."

Colin smiled and stared at Amanda. "Ah, no problem. Of course, having a knockout beauty sitting on me might lead to me getting a little, shall we say, aroused."

"Thank you," Amanda said sincerely as she placed her hand on Colin's lap. "You can raise the flagship any time you want. I rather enjoy the rear stimulation, as we found out last night." Everyone giggled.

"So any desires to see anything along the lines of a mother nature type around here before we go?" Leanne asked.

"I wanted to see the Great Trees Trail on Meares Island," Colin said. "We've got to get a water taxi down at the docks and take it over to a raised trail, so we don't need any hiking shoes or anything. You good with that?"

"Yes," she said, looking at her and Colin. Today she seemed shy, quiet, and nearly insecure. Perhaps the alcohol had loosened Amanda more than Leanne realized. Or she'd been storing up her feelings for a long time like some people do and later regret what they'd done.

"Okay, you lead the way then, my good man."

****

A couple of hours later, they walked among the giant cedars, some over fifty feet around, although stunted their tops broken many times from the high winds and storms that tore over the coast, looking like some kind of mystical witching trees. Colin walked ahead, in awe of the place, while a subdued Amanda walked quietly beside Leanne. It was obvious there was a lot going through her head, probably raised from last night.

"Amanda, can I ask you something? Do you like Colin?"

"Yes, Leanne. He's absolutely dead handsome. Too bad he's your boyfriend. I don't suppose you've room for a permanent third partner?"

"Before I respond to that, can I ask, last night you seemed to enjoy being my lover more than being with a man. Was it just the booze that had made you more adventurous? Or do you enjoy being with men more?"

Amanda stopped walking and looked Leanne in the eyes. "If I'm to be very honest, I like being with a guy more. Colin is amazing, but I need to find a man who will be okay with letting me have a woman once in a while. Either that or I find a woman that lets me have a guy sometimes. I'm a bit confused, I think what I'm trying to say—"

"Is that part of you desires being with a woman. Especially one that takes control and dominates you."

"Oh God, yes, that is what my gym teacher did with me."

"Tell me, I'm curious to know."

Colin ran back up to them. "The water taxi is returning." The three sat on the bench while waiting for the water taxi to arrive. "I'd love to hear this story as well."

"I don't remember how it happened. I remember being in her office after school. She was mad because I'd blown a couple of cheerleading routines and before I knew it, she had me over her knees. Spanking me. Only the pain was making me horny. I remember her hands rubbing my rear. Me moaning and saying something crazy like, 'Is it wrong that this is also turning me on?' She pulled down my panties and continued to spank me.

"I was getting so aroused. She asked me if I liked her hand on my ass. I said yes, in a state of great desire. I remember her fondling my rear and saying how delicious it looked all reddened before she slipped her hand between my legs and found my pussy sopping wet. Before I knew it, she had one hand fingering me and the other fondling my breasts. Like you did to me last night. I came so quickly. I'd never been like that with any of the guys I went out with. In fact, I never came with most of them."

Leanne put her arm around Amanda. "And then?"

"Like you last night, she made me get before her on my knees and eat her out. I couldn't believe how much I enjoyed doing that. Sorry, Colin, but something about a woman dominating me sets off some deep need. A fantasy that I never thought I'd enjoy again until I tried it last night."

"Like me taking your ass. You really enjoy being her submissive lover?" Colin pondered.

"Yes, and we made love many times after that. She

usually liked being in control, spanking me, or tying me up. I liked her to take me, make me submit to her, being out of control. My life had been so controlled and safe before I met her. So when you did the same to me, Leanne, I was so aroused. I can't help it. I don't know what to do. I don't think there's a man out there who would want me, and I know I wouldn't be happy either. It stinks, I really don't know what to do."

She began to sob into her hands. Colin moved immediately to comfort her. "Linda, the teacher, moved to another province at the end of the term and all of my nights in the last three years have been spent either working or being by myself. How many nights I've masturbated in bed, fantasizing about being her submissive lover again, wanting to be dominated. I only decided to go out with my work friends last night as a way of getting out. Don't know why I did, but I'm glad I did, and when I saw you, Leanne, you looked so much like Linda. I only know I'd do anything to be with you. So when you walked up to me, I was speechless." She squeezed Leanne's hand. "When you said you wanted me as well, I think I nearly wet myself."

Leanne stared at Colin. "So here's the truth, I only picked up Colin as a way of having company on my way to Banff for an Arts Course. We're not an item. My husband had died and I needed someone to get over it. Colin has only been my male escort for the last couple of days."

"It's true." He smiled at the two of them. "Likewise, Leanne, I found you stunning. I've always wanted to be with a redhead and thought I'd love to be her boy-toy for a few days, no commitments other than company for each other and hot sex at night. That was our agreement. It's okay, Leanne. I don't think I'm old enough for you. There's lots I want to do yet. My parents want to retire soon and I wouldn't mind taking over their restaurant on Cannon Beach someday. Part of my education is taking business studies and chef classes."

Amanda stared at him and her. "So you two aren't really a thing."

"No," they both responded. "After tomorrow, I'm off, I'm an American. I live in California, and I've got a real estate business to run in Hollywood," Leanne added. "He's great and fantastic in bed, but like he said, just my hired stud for the time being."

Colin looked at Leanne first and then at Amanda. "So if I can be honest while we're puking our guts out here...Amanda, I find you absolutely gorgeous, and I wouldn't have a problem if you were with me bringing other women into the picture. Last night went so far past my greatest fantasies, I can't even begin to explain it. I'd love to see you some more. Hell, I'd even help you find another woman to satisfy those lesbian domination cravings."

She stared at him. "Really, you'd be okay with that? Here I thought I was so weird and messed up."

"God, I'm getting hard just thinking of it." He leaned over and kissed her. "Me too, I mean wet."

Leanne smiled. Okay the surprises seemed to be ongoing on this trip. Expect the frigging unexpected, Sam was right. She had just helped two unhappy people get together and maybe, just maybe, they'd become a couple, have babies, two point five kids and a motor home to go to Mexico every summer. Oh, she could only wish, like her someday.

The ding of the approaching water taxi bouncing along the waves broke their tableau.

As they boarded, Leanne couldn't help but wonder how a woman as beautiful as Amanda could be so shy and lacking confidence. Still, maybe her getting together with Colin had led to this, the two of them becoming an item. Coincidences, who'd have thought?

If nothing else, it was a few nights of great sex and wonderful memories.

****

The trip in from Tofino had been calm, they visited the Cathedral grove outside of Port Alberni again. It was hard to imagine trees that massive. Leanne had seen the Redwoods of California and these towered nearly as high. It was hard to imagine what this country was like before so much was cut down. To watch the two of them holding hands was also wonderful, something so innocent and sweet, after all the kinkiness they had wallowed in.

The ferry ride on the BC ferry to Horseshoe Bay from Nanaimo was quiet as well. Colin and Amanda disappeared for quite a while to check out the waves and possible whale sightings. Leanne smiled to herself. They were obviously very keen on each other and that was okay with her. She'd gotten what she wanted with him along and more. Amanda was an unexpected bonus. Well, actually, the last three days were all unexpected bonus distractions. Ones that had gotten her out of her funk over Ben and her dad. That seemed like another lifetime ago.

She stared at the headlines of the BC Province newspaper, *Latest burning of Hell's Angel's Clubhouse has the city of Vancouver nervous. Many are asking, is this the beginning of a drug war? And is it related to the recent Death of Vancouver's Mayor, found brutally slain by the Pauline Johnson memorial in Stanley Park Last Week?*

Colin stared at the paper and the woman leading a group of reporters, as he sat down. "Hey, I know that lady that's Carol Ainsworth, my aunt, she was just made a Vancouver detective."

"Well, I think she looks like she's heading this case and I hate to say it, in deep shit right about now. Might be wise to not speed through the city, I don't think anyone's in a laughing mood."

Amanda giggled. "It's okay, at least here in Canada, we don't shoot first and ask questions later."

"Oh yeah." Leanne grimaced. "No guns, just free drugs for all the heroin addicts, I just read on another page while you two were, quote, viewing the dolphins and whales, unquote.

Not sure which country is more messed up."

Colin hugged Amanda. "Right about now, don't care."

Leanne smiled. "I can see why, hugging that tasty morsel."

"Well if he doesn't mind I could help settle a little of your hungers in the washroom, my mistress." Amanda laughed.

"Sorry, I'm definitely a landlubber, the only rocking I like to do is in the bedroom." They all laughed.

Later, outside an older bungalow in West Vancouver, the three got out. They were dropping Amanda off first. Colin lived only a few miles along the coast in the expensive British Properties area. His parents had done very well in life, that was obvious.

Amanda hugged Leanne and gave her a big kiss on the lips. Her well-endowed chest crushed against Leanne. A subtle thrill ran through her at the memory of those breasts naked in her hands and on her lips. "Thanks for everything, and if you ever come up this way again and need a woman to dominate, call me." She smiled shyly. "That was amazing. Not to mention you hooked me up with this gorgeous man." She hugged Colin. "For that, I shall be forever grateful."

Amanda turned to Colin. "You are just the most amazing man this woman could have ever met. I didn't think I could find anyone that would like me just the way I am. Thank you. I'll be ready on Saturday night at six."

"Can't wait." He leaned over and kissed her long and hard. Leanne supposed she should be jealous in some way, but she wasn't. His company the last few days was delicious and a wonderful boost to her ego. Leanne knew he wasn't right for her, as a long-term partner. His attitude to life, while fresh, was a little too naive. She needed a partner with a more mature outlook on life or perhaps a woman like her friends, Sam and Janice, with complete openness in their relationship. And besides, trying to hook up with anyone right now would be more like rebound. Still, it was great to have a young stud to escort her around and his willingness to be with her and fulfill her sexual desires was more than a wonderful distraction to her holiday journey. Plus, he was a great tour guide.

Colin climbed back in the BMW. Leanne could see the bulge beginning in his tight jeans.

"Sorry, I hope you're okay with me asking her

out."

"I'm more than okay. If our getting together led you to find a great woman and also helping her get a wonderful, understanding man in her life, then it was all worth it."

"Thanks, we're going to go out clubbing this weekend, and as I said to her, we'll look for a woman for her and if we don't find one, it'll just be the two of us having our own party. Either way is great. I got to say, Leanne, you are an inspiration to me. These last couple of days have been an unbelievable experience. I shall never forget you. Thanks, and in the future, if there's anything I can do for you, let me know. Especially if you need a male stud escort for a weekend." He laughed.

Leanne beamed back. "You'll be the first to call or if I have the desire to put your sexy girlfriend over my knees and spank her?"

"Oh yeah, especially that. That was the hottest thing I've ever been involved in. Again, thanks." He leaned over and gave her a deep kiss.

She had both their phone numbers. Who knew? Maybe a trip up to Vancouver in the future could be a pleasant idea. "And thanks for the company. You've made this former grieving woman get on with her life. Thanks. Oh, and as I mentioned earlier, if you ever need help with the restaurant or something, I could loan you some money."

"Thanks, I don't usually mix money and pleasure. But the offer is wonderful."

Leanne fired up the BMW and hit the throttle after punching in the coordinates for Banff, Alberta on her

GPS. She turned on the music and with a smile on her face drove onto the TransCanada highway.

Chapter Five

Two days later she reached Banff. The Canadian Rockies were amazing. Snow-capped mountains towering into the sky, she'd stopped overnight at a small city called Revelstoke. Mostly a logging town and simply retired to her hotel room. She never thought she'd say it, but it was nice to be alone in her bed. Not something she really ever thought she'd enjoy, but was getting used to it.

On the way into Banff, she had to pass Lake Louise and took a slight detour to view the lake and the hotel. Incredibly as she pulled out her print, it hadn't changed the slightest. The same view of turquoise waters, Mt. Victoria in the distance as her mom had seen. Somehow it made her small and insignificant to realize that long after she was dead someone else could be holding this nearly a hundred-year-old print and viewing the same view. Eternal mountains, well at least to humans.

She could have booked a few nights into the Banff Arts Center. The online reviews were amazing. Leanne had picked a couple of art classes to attend. Instead, she picked the posh Fairmount Banff Springs Hotel, as it was called now. One of the grand hotels built along the new rail line meant to attract rich customers to Canada and the Rockies back in the days when this country was new and unexplored. She stared up at the sheer cliff edge of Mt. Rundle before her. In the valley below the

Bow River wound its way past the Banff Springs golf course. "What a fantastic view." She beamed from her hotel window.

****

When she went to register for her Arts classes at the Banff Center, there was a bulletin board notice about an Erotic

Naked Study Drawing class in the Painter's Studio of the private Mountain Artists Colony, 'not for the timid of heart' it stated. She phoned and a sultry voice answered the phone. Introducing herself as Vesper, she described how it was expected that each person involved would get naked and pose for the class, either by themselves or most likely with someone else, while the others drew them.

"Count me in," she answered. After everything that had happened on this trip and in the last few months of her life with work and the bizarre Hollywood crowd, this seemed somehow tame.

****

Janice called her up that night as she lay sipping wine in her room. Mt. Rundle towered up behind the hotel. Below the golf course and the Bow River ambled by. "I was going to text, but I thought I'd try to reach you in person. You ain't going to believe what happened to me last night. It was the weirdest and most erotic night I ever had."

"After my last couple of nights I'd say you'd have a hard time topping my experience, but go ahead, you first," Leanne responded, still pleasantly sore as she rose in her bed. Sun streaming in over the view of Mt. Rundle Mountain.

"Well, you remember Jenny Carstairs who played

126

Galaxy Girl in that tacky eighties short-run TV series? A spin-off from the Wonder Woman shows."

"Yes, very curvy and well built. If I remember, she'd talked about perhaps purchasing some property just before I left. She was interested in my extra services, but she didn't let me know what her secret desire was before I left."

"I talked to her and what she asked for I thought was a little bizarre, not really being a fan of any TV show and a bit before my time. She said she did a scene in one of her shows where she'd been abducted and tied up by a villainess. At the time she thought she was happily married and purely straight. Only in reality, the lady playing the villainess asked her if she'd go back to her trailer, where she wanted to tie her up for real and have her way with her. Miss Carstairs said that scene always haunted her and fed some sort of dark fantasy of hers."

"So you agreed to be a villainess that ties up the indestructible Galaxy Girl."

"No, she wanted me to be Galaxy Girl and Jenny played the villainess, Black Spider. She wanted to be the evil one and I had to stay in character the whole time in order to create the true effect of the scene. I was thinking one of those weird fan convention things."

"Oh, sounds weird and kinky already."

"Yeah, I thought so, only it gets stranger. After I dressed in the Galaxy Girl outfit and she returned in her sheer black outfit, with a large spider etched crawling over her massive breasts, she offered me some herbal tea. She said it would help to arouse the senses, I innocently drank it. Only what was in there I don't know, it wiped me out. Some sort of hallucinogenic drug, don't know what it was but I passed out."

"She stoned you, really? This is beginning to sound sexy already."

"Yup, I thought so, until I came to tied up and helpless in a chair."

Leanne shifted in the bed. "Continue with all the descriptions, this sounds like someone we kidnapped once."

"And had our way with. Oh, yes, I was totally in her control. I could barely talk, let alone resist or get up and walk. While I was conscious, the drug had still left me very lethargic and limp.

"All I remember was she looked into my dilated eyes. 'I see my spider's venom potion has begun to take effect. You see, Ms. Galaxy, it saps your strength, but later begins to arouse the senses. You, my law-abiding do-gooder are now my helpless prey.'

"I tried to lift my arms and even though I was tied to the chair, could barely flex my fingers.

"She raked her long fingernails along my arms and leaned in to lick my neck.

"'I do like helpless prey to play with.'

"I gasped, so hot, so hot. Leanne, I was totally under her control. I didn't expect that and worse I wasn't sure if she was totally sane or some crazy homicidal slasher."

"I gather you're not covered in Band-Aids, so she wasn't totally bananas. Do continue, I'm getting very aroused just thinking about it."

"Thanks for the concern. For a few moments, I thought she'd set me up for some kind of grisly slaughter, like in the movies.

"'I see the effects are very strong in you.' The

Black Spider said next, 'I think it is safe to say you are totally in my control. Now I can imagine a busy person of your nature, fighting crime, and saving lives doesn't have much time for a personal life. Do you, Ms. Galaxy?'

"'No,' I gasped as she moved behind me, I was barely able to speak. Her breath hot on my neck, her tongue licking the length of my neck a few times like I was some sort of delicious treat.

"'Oh, I do like the taste of helpless prey.' She moved to stand before me and took off her Black Spider's outfit to reveal a black fifties type of corset with a small green spider emblem on the front, her breasts hung over the top partly suspended and even though she had a suspender holding up black stockings she wore no panties. Only a thick black bush. Her breasts had huge aureole surrounding large dark nipples. I remember getting aroused just staring at her. She looked so commanding, so dominant.

"'So you see, I've admired you for a long time. Always wondered what you must do, if anything, to shall we say, get off in your spare time.'

"All I could do was gasp as she moved behind me again and ran those soft breasts against my back. Her tongue returned to licking my neck and gently biting and sucking my skin like some dormant vampire.

"'I figured such a dominant type of superheroine must have a partner at night and if not you must be awfully stressed out, uptight. So you see, I've captured you, not to do you in, but to do you. I want you to remember me every night after tonight. Probably fantasize about me, getting yourself off. Masturbating to the night when you were my helpless prey and all the filthy things we did together.'

"'You're crazy, Black Spider.' I finally blurted out, in quite the effort. She just continued nibbling on my neck, sending shivers down to my crotch. I think she was right about that potion of hers, while making me weak and lethargic, it also contained some sort of aphrodisiac.

"'Yes, that's what makes me the evil one. You on the other hand are my victim.' She slid down the top strands of my outfit exposing my breasts, openly fondling them. My nipples were already hard and rudely sticking out.

"'Very hard, very erect. Ms. Galaxy, who'd have known you've such pointy nipples.'

"From behind she reached around and continued to openly fondle my breasts rolling my throbbing nipples hard between her fingers, pulling on them. All I could do was moan, so aroused. Whatever was in her tea she was right, it had begun to set every nerve I had on fire, like being prickled by millions of ants crawling over me with needles on their feet, that sort of raw stimulation.

"'I think my spider's venom is doing its job, sensitizing all of your nerve endings. I've always wanted to do this to you, my heroine. Oh, and this.' With one hand, she grabbed my face and shoved her tongue down my throat, raping my mouth with her tongue like a man would with his hard cock. I surrendered to her, my body was beginning to turn to fire. Knowing I was helpless, she returned to fondling my breasts with one hand while the other held my head to her as she deep-tongued me. I remember moaning, her hand pinching and squeezing my nipples. Time seemed to slow down, every slither of her tongue began to feel like long moments of pleasure, each twist of my nipples exquisite. I'd probably have cum before too long if she continued. Time stretching away into long moments of total and complete surrender."

"Oh yeah, she definitely stoned you," Leanne interrupted.

"I may have to buy the series in order to catch that episode."

"I've been stoned, there was some sort of aphrodisiac in that tea, that set all my nerves raw and tender."

"Interesting, continue."

"The Black Spider said, 'Now do you think it fair that yours are the only ones that get pleasured? Especially when mine are so much larger.'

"'No,' was all I could groan as her fingers continued to sensitize my nipples, twirling them in her fingers. She bent lower and began to suck each nipple, biting more than lightly on them. I screamed, either in pain or ecstasy, couldn't tell you which. Probably both. She came around to the front of me and sat on my lap, spreading her legs around me, like a spider trapping her prey.

"'Now be a good superheroine and return the favor.' She put one hand behind my head and held her breast to my lips. I began to suck and lick her tit like my life depended on it and at the time I thought it might. I was hungry to satisfy her.

"'Ah, you've no idea how long I've waited for you to do that to me, Galaxy Girl, and the night has just begun.' She lifted my face and deep kissed me again. 'I think you like sucking on these massive tits of mine.'

"I tried to say no, but couldn't, all I could think of

was to continue sucking on those overly large nipples of hers. 'I do,' was all I could muster as she returned her other breast to my mouth and I eagerly sucked and licked away. 'Oh baby, you definitely like sucking on these breasts. I always thought you'd enjoy the pleasures of another woman. I wondered if you had a dyke streak in you, Ms. Galaxy.' She pulled her breast away. My lips were making sucking sounds in the air. 'So helpless, so hungry, so mine.' She raped my mouth with her tongue again and sucked her way down my throat.

"'Yes,' I gasped. She was such a dominating lesbian, even Sam didn't do things that arousing or forceful."

"Maybe I'll have to have a couple of hero outfits made up for Halloween." Leanne gasped, her fingers already stoking herself at the thought.

"Don't you dare!"

"Now what did she do next? You're getting me so wet I'm playing with myself. Never thought phone sex could be so arousing."

"You wet? I was virtually panting.

"'Now, my aroused heroine. Time for a little discipline, like I demand of all that serve me. After all, the Black Spider is known to devour her prey and I'll bet you'd like to be devoured right about now, don't you?'

"'Please.' I begged as she pinched my left nipple again. She reached into her hair and unclipped what I thought was just to keep her hair back. Two clamps attached to a silver chain. I knew what they were for as she released them and holding hair wasn't their purpose.

"'Now, my helpless heroine, a little pain to make you very aware of who is in charge and keep you very eager to satisfy me.' She lifted my left breast and slowly placed the nipple clamp on it. I involuntarily moaned as she attached the other one to my second breast. 'Now I believe my right nipple is suffering from lack of attention.'

"Fire seared through me as my nipples screamed in pain. She tugged me by the chain to her awaiting breast. I kissed and sucked on it like a starving child. The clamps sent searing pain through me, all the way to my crotch.

"'Most delicious. I do believe you enjoy being tied up and helpless, out of control. Who'd have thought the great Galaxy Girl would be so eager to pleasure me.'

"She held my mouth to her breast and then the other. Alternating with deep tonguing my mouth. Obviously working herself up. I was nearly slobbering, so totally aroused at being used by her—a slave to her desires.

"'I love it when you let go, Ms. Galaxy. How long has it been since you've cum? I'll bet too long.' As she kissed me again she slid her hand down between us and cupped my pussy through the uniform. I ground myself against her hand. The urge to get off, so compelling. It was all I could think of. 'So moist. I do believe you're enjoying this.'

"I merely nodded, sucking on her long tongue wishing it were between my legs as her fingers slide through my wet hunger. 'Now, missy, I do believe it's time for you to do your good deed for the day and relieve me of my distress. And I know how much you like to help those in distress.' She lifted her fingers to my mouth. Without being told what to do, I sucked my own muskiness from her fingers like a starving dog offered a bone.

"'Very nice and hungry to service your master, aren't you, Galaxy Girl.' I looked at her and nodded, so on the edge of needing to orgasm, I was shaking.

"She got up and untied my hands from the chair and retied them behind my back. Making my breasts jut out. She tugged on the chain, and I moaned in delirium, so delicious the searing pain. Untying my legs she pushed me to my knees.

"'Time, my do-gooder to perform your good deed of the day.' She lifted one leg and placed it on the chair. I stared into her thick black wet bush and licked my lips. 'You'll always remember the day you were forced to eat the Black Spider's hairy pussy and know that it was you that aroused it. Only I don't think I'm really forcing you anymore, am I?'

"'No.'

"'Say it.'

"'I want to satisfy you with my mouth. I want to eat your pussy more than anything else.

"'That's a good superheroine. Doing as she's told. Now come to service your new mistress.'

"I moved my head forward and kissed that luscious black bush. My tongue slid between her wetness, slurping with delight. Her muskiness washing over me.

"'Slowly, I like my women to lick me slowly' and as I begin to cum' suck on my clit. Understand?' She tugged on the chain attached to my nipples as she pulled my head away. I screamed a little.

"'Yes, my evil mistress,' I mumbled into her thick forest of black pubic hair as she shoved my face back into that garden of desire.

"The Black Spider arched her back, moaning as I licked her labia lips and began to tongue her opening. I ran my tongue slowly along her slit. The muskiness washed over me. She was so aroused she began to buck involuntarily over my mouth. Humping my face. She'd done this many times before with other women, I was sure. I was so hungry to bring her to an orgasm, to service this dominant villain.

"'Oh, it's starting far too quickly. You are good, I think you've satisfied other women before, my hungry heroine. Now, suck on my clit, softly.'

"I latched onto her engorged clit and sucked on it like a small cock. The Black Spider cried out as she held my face into her pubic mound, humping my face as she came. She shuddered again and again, rubbing her cunt over my face and mouth, before pulling away.

"'Oh very delicious, Ms. Galaxy. Usually my first one isn't that strong. I think you're in for a long night of pleasuring me with that wonderful mouth and tongue. I'll watch the news knowing on every interview or shot of you, that those wonderful lips licked me to orgasm after orgasm.'

"She pulled me up with the chain and frenched me again. This time licking my lips. 'Or the night when my pussy juices flowed from your lips down your chin.'

"'You're evil.'

"'I think we're in total agreement on that. But it's time you wore some more of my juices and service the last orifice I desire your mouth on, my helpless heroine.'

"'No,' I gasped as she shoved me to the ground and laid me flat, hands trapped behind my back.

"She got on top of me backward and slapped my legs apart hard with her hands. I could barely lift my legs, the drugs still strong in me. 'Now we'll see if you can do that again with your wonderful mouth. Only I want you to kiss my anus first and begin to fuck me with that delicious tongue. And if you don't this will be your reward.' She smacked my exposed pussy hard with her hand several times.

"I cried out, so aroused, nearly on the edge of my own orgasm. 'Please, Black Spider, I want to lick your ass. I need to cum, so close,' I moaned nearly coming.

"'I can tell. I thought you'd see it my way.' One of her fingers slipped between my moist lips. I moaned uncontrollably, shuddering and thrusting myself to her hand pleasuring me.

"She leaned over my pussy and breathed in my musky aromas. I opened my eyes and saw her brown hole over my mouth.

"'Ah, breathe in that hunger to pleasure your mistress.'

"I reached out with my tongue and licked the length of her anus. Then began the slow licking and sucking of her rear slit. Finally my tongue teased her anal cavity. I slid it inside as far as I could. She began to hump my tongue and groaned. 'The great Galaxy Girl, fucking my ass with her tongue.' She moaned again before shifting her body higher. 'Suck my clit again, my hungry dutiful lesbian slave.'

"I began to suck her clit as she reached between my legs and vigorously fingered me. Occasionally stopping to slap my pussy.

"'Oh, I'm coming again, you wonderful bitch.'

"She began to shudder and dropped her face to

between my legs and licked my pussy and sucked on my clit. I'd been held on the edge so long almost immediately I exploded in convulsions as I thrust myself on her face. We kept sucking and licking, until exhausted. I haven't had many multiple orgasms, but I did that night and I think she did as well. Even with Sam it rarely got that intense.

"Finally Black Spider rolled off me. 'Didn't know you had that in you, did you, Galaxy Girl?'

"I could barely move let alone talk as the orgasms still sent shivers through me and the drugs while weakening still had me feeling lethargic.

"She snapped her fingers twice. 'Oh, boys.'

"Two men dressed in black outfits, with green spiders on their chests and full face masks entered. Their arousal quite evident from the bulges sticking out of their outfits. They must have been watching us the whole time. 'Now finish yourselves off, Galaxy Girl is yours to use.'

"They rolled me on my stomach and untied my hands. 'On your knees,' one commanded. I could barely move but I did as they wanted me. One opened his black spandex crotch area and out sprang his cock. 'Suck me,' he ordered and as I did the other shoved his cock into me from behind. I was so sensitive from all the orgasms I could do little but submit to the men. The Black Spider walked up and began to slap my ass as the men fucked me, watching me being stuffed by their cocks.

"'How humiliated is Galaxy Girl now?'

"I could only moan as one man came and a minute later the other. I virtually collapsed in a whimpering wreck as they withdrew their throbbing cocks. The

Black Spider pulled a cloth from her pocket and a vial. She dabbed it on the cloth and held it to my nose. 'Good night, Galaxy Girl.'

"She must have had chloroform, one breath and I passed out. When I came to I was in my car again fully dressed in my normal clothes as if I'd dreamed it.

"Only a note on the dash said, *Thanks for the most intense night of my life. I always wanted to be the bad ass. Anytime you want to get captured again, call me.* Except for the headache from the drugs I thought it was all a bad dream, until I moved to put on my seatbelt and felt the tug of the nipple clamps, the bitch had left them on me. God, my nipples are so sore and my butt still aches from her slaps, not to mention the rest of me. But you know what, sometimes I think it's good when the villainess wins."

Leanne gasped as her fingers flew over her clit. She was getting close to coming herself. "Leaving the clamps on you under your clothes, nice touch."

"Yeah, the bitch. God, some people have the wildest fantasies and imaginations. I don't think I could ever pick up a comic book without blushing."

"And I need to hang up now because I'm about to cum myself. Still got those clamps?"

"Yes. Would you like me to use those on you some night?"

"Definitely. Wish you were here to put them on me now and finish me off. You definitely win. I just managed to pick up a handsome young stud for the last few days and a hot cheerleader type woman about his age to have a threesome with."

"Oh, tell me about it," Janice asked, her voice low. Leanne could tell she also was playing with herself.

Leanne told her about her adventures in explicit detail. Both ladies were soon moaning to each other over the phone. "So she loved being your little slave girl and now they're getting together. Funny way to begin a relationship."

"Yup. Oh, I'm so close."

"So am I."

They both moaned, "I gotta go," at the same time.

****

"These are our outdoor kilns, where we fire most of our pottery," the sultry-voiced Vesper said as she showed Leanne around the Arts Center. She wanted to meet Vesper and get a feel for the Erotic Arts Class before attending. Leanne breathed deeply of the fresh clean Banff mountain air. The Bow River flowed far below, a deep, unsoiled turquoise.

Vesper sauntered up to her. "Breathtaking, isn't it?" The tall brunette reminded her of Sam, except for the two braids of hair on her left side. She reminded Leanne of someone slightly out of sync from the sixties. The erotic thought of Sam's seduction tingled through her mind quickly as Vesper looked her up and down. Someone with her free-spirited mind was probably into much more than just males, or at least she hoped.

"So this experimental erotic drawing class on Saturday, can you give me some more details?"

Vesper leaned into her. "There'll be about a dozen people. The expectation is you may have to get naked and be a still-life model, usually with someone else. That is why I said it is a bit risqué and with everyone getting naked, who knows what will happen later. Each person will get up with someone else I pick, others draw you. Held on Saturday evening, the art colony is closed to the public and it'll be just us in class at the private Painter's Studio," Vesper whispered softly in her ear. "I'd love to see you there and naked."

A thrill ran through her as Vesper described what the session would be about. Leanne looked her in the eye. "I'd love to partake." She was more than interested in partaking of Vesper as well. She reminded Leanne of a Raven-haired Sam, only with more curves and with that look in her eyes that told her, like Colin had, that she wanted her.

****

Vesper stood on the dais at the front of the group. They'd all had time to have a glass of wine and relax before their easels.

"Now, if any of you want to say no at any time, and that goes for all of you. That's okay, but remember being an artist means living on the edge of your comfort zone where creativity and risk collide. So be unreasonable with yourselves and what you expect to happen. Throw all of your inhibitions in the closet, like your clothes in the back room."

They'd all stripped down and covered themselves with bathrobes before entering the room.

With that, she whipped off her robe and threw it over her shoulder. She stood naked before the collected gasps of the group and turned with a seductive pose, one hand on hip. "You've fifteen minutes to draw, begin."

Leanne stared at her a moment. The woman was luscious. Her breasts about a 38D that sagged not in the least. Her hips, full and wonderfully curved, hid the old-fashioned full bush, very sixties hippy looking, as raven-colored as her braided hair.

Leanne licked her lips before beginning to scribble away. Her picture had Vesper standing commanding, with Leanne on her knees before her, pleasuring her.

She hoped Vesper viewed these after. Living on the edge of reason was where she'd been these last couple of weeks, with the trip to the hotel, Colin, Amanda, and now this class. "Stop when you can," Vesper uttered.

She pulled up a chair to the raised platform and sat on it. For all to view, she spread her legs open and ran one hand down between, while with the other she squeezed one of her nipples. It hardened under the pressure as she moaned. "Now, start drawing again, same picture or a fresh one, whatever triggers your compulsions." She ran her fingers over her clit, obviously turned on by being naked and masturbating herself to the full view of the class.

After quiet furious minutes where only lead sang over paper. She erupted again. "Okay, stop and finish up as best as you can. The idea is to get the basics down and you can finish the rest later. Now, as you can see, I brook no prisoners." Vesper laughed. "I won't question why if anyone wants to leave. Go now, a full refund is available for the next twenty seconds, now that you can see where this class is capable of going.

She stared at the clock and waited. No one stood up.

Leanne could already feel wetness between her legs. She wasn't sure if this was more about sex than drawing, but she was open to both and really open to Vesper.

"Okay, I've read your files and there's a reason I ask so many questions regarding my class. I'm trying to get a sense of what turns you on, your hidden desires."

She put her robe back on and got off the dais, walking around the room until she stood at the back. "Because putting each of you on the edge of risk awakens desires that can be incredible for the rest of us to try and capture on print and in our imaginations. Passion, unbridled, when caught at the right moment is what artists sometimes try to capture and experience at least once in their lives."

She let the words sink in before continuing, "And trust me, more than one couple has emailed me to say thank you for introducing them to each other and got married down the road, or living together I call that the bonus to this class, a tip shall we say."

"Each couple will be on the dais for twenty minutes in two different poses each. First, I'll call up Brindi and Hans."

Leanne thought it curious who she called out first. Hans was a blonde-haired, slightly reddish goateed Norwegian who had a large vee-shaped upper body build with a massive chest and stood a little over six foot. She'd have guessed he did a lot of weights in his spare time. She wondered how Hans could remotely be into any drawings with the size of his hands, which were like bear paws. Brindi was a tiny Chinese girl, small, petite, with the oriental black straight hair and so mousy looking, she also didn't look the artistic type, more like an accountant.

"Both take off your robes and for this first set, strip naked." Brindi barely reached Hans' belly button as she pulled off her panties. Hans had already taken all of his clothes off and stood arms folded on his chest, rather proud looking, with a large physique, powerful shoulders, thick pecs—he obviously worked out a lot.

He had that ancient Viking look to him and Leanne could see why he stood with such pride. His uncut cock hung free; soft it was a good eight inches. What surprised her was its girth. More big around than any man she'd seen hard, what would it be like engorged with blood and hunger?

Vesper moved around the couple pondering on how to pose them. The Chinese girl's eyes seemed fixated at the sight of Han's very thick cock. "Brindi, I see you're rather taken with our very well-endowed Scandinavian."

"I've never seen a Caucasian, organ, ah, penis. It's so large," she managed to gasp, transfixed at the man's third leg.

"Take your place before Hans on your knees," Vesper commanded.

He wouldn't be ashamed hanging that meaty stick around in front of any black man, if the stereotype were to be believed, Leanne thought. She hadn't been with one yet, but most of her friends had said it was true. They were built like tree trunks, and Hans had one hell of an oak timber on him.

Brindi gulped as she stared at his massive cock, sinking to her knees. "You are about to service him with your mouth. Open your mouth slightly and move close to him."

Brindi's eyes opened up in shock and somewhere, Leanne could see crossing her mind, the desire to have a penis that large in her. It was obvious she'd never seen a man's organ that close or that large. "Legs apart. You are about to take his cock in your mouth, make it come alive, thicken harden. Fill your mouth."

Brindi's eyes bulged. She was in awe of this man's

flaccid girth. Her lips wavered. Leanne could see the desire cross her eyes and the fear, maybe she couldn't even get her lips around his uncut head. It was plain she wanted to suck on that man's cock. Her hidden desires, cravings. Vesper probably knew something about this tiny oriental from her notes. She had definitely hit that raw edge of Brindi's comfort zone.

"Open your mouth, another hand between your legs."

She moaned, touching herself, overcome in her wanting to suck in this man's very thick cock, scant inches from her wanting mouth. Whatever Vesper knew about this girl, she knew the sight of Han's enormous cock was driving Brindi well past her limits of decency. Her fingers stroked between her legs. His cock begging for her wet mouth. Oh, yes, there was a scene of sheer erotic longing building here.

The soft rub of pencil and water paints echoed as filtered sunlight cast a golden glow across the two on the dais. Hans, Leanne could tell, struggled to keep himself soft, or at least semi-flaccid as they heard Brindi's warm breath, now coming in ragged shorter bursts. Leanne had no doubt that if this was allowed to continue long enough she'd finger herself to orgasm without touching or tasting him. This was such an erotic scene. But that was the idea. Her pencil flew across the pad. Several minutes later, as time was running out, Brindi began to pant, fingers rubbing between her legs, obviously getting close.

"Time, quickly finish your strokes while I set these two up for the second scene. Now, Brindi, you seem rather aroused at the sight of his big cock."

"Yes, teacher. I've never seen a Caucasian male

penis before. It's so big."

"Well, I can assure you that not all white males are built like our Norwegian friend here. So am I to guess that having something that large inside of you would be a huge turn-on?"

Her eyes bulged, telling the crowd all they needed to hear.

"I couldn't…he's so…"

Vesper pulled up a chair. "Willing to try?"

Brindi stared at Hans' cock already beginning to harden at the suggestion. She gulped loudly. "Get on the chair, butt in the air, arms on the back. He's going to enter you from behind. Stuff himself slowly into you pretending to fuck you. You'll have to keep still for the pose. Can you do that?"

Brindi looked mortified as she turned around, shaking without speaking a word. Hans was hardening at the thought. Whatever she or Leanne thought this course was about or would be like, this wasn't it.

"If you need to, Hans, stroke yourself." He stroked himself at the sight of the tiny dark pussy offered to him. To enter something that tiny and obviously tight didn't take him long to be throbbing hard.

"Here, put this condom on, Hans. Now, while he's doing that, are you wet, Brindi, or should I have Hans assist in getting you ready?"

"Very wet, teacher." Her words a mere whisper. The fear and desire ran rampant through her eyes.

"Hang on to the chair as Hans enters you."

Hans opened her lips and slowly placed his cock to her and pushed into the tiny Asian girl. She groaned deeply, lost in the man stuffing himself inside her, babbles in some foreign language bubbled from her lips.

"Oh, so tight."

"If he goes soft use your vaginal muscles to work him."

Hans moaned. "You won't have to worry about that. She's the tightest pussy I've ever been in. God, so tight."

"He's splitting me," she cried out, sheer lust forcing her eyes closed.

"Now draw," Vesper said as Brindi bit on her lip, her face in inscrutable ecstasy, trying to keep still when it was obvious to all she wanted to be impaling herself on his massive cock. Fighting to keep still as his large hardness slid slowly in and out of her.

Brindi let out a moan as the rush of pencils filled the air. Vesper walked up to her. "Tell me what's going through your head. It will help the others to draw."

"So big, he's splitting me. His penis is throbbing, I'm throbbing. So filled." Sweat rolled down her face.

Hans groaned. "She's…" He moaned. "…she's stroking my dick with her tight muscles."

"Good girl. That's tantric sex, if you didn't know. Now continue to stroke him, if you or Hans cums, that's okay. Just don't move." Vesper smiled to the class, as pencils flew over paper.

Brindi grunted something sounding Oriental, lost in the sensations. A couple of minutes later she softly cried out. Her body going limp. "So sorry, teacher, I tried to hold it to the end. I failed," she cried out.

"Well, what do you think, Hans, is it fair that only one of you gets a release?"

He shook his head.

"Very slowly, if you can move in and out."

"So wet," he gasped as he pulled back, "and tight."

"So big," Brindi cried as he pushed himself forward and closed her eyes. She began to shudder, her lips mumbling away as it was obvious another orgasm was building inside. Hans held her thin olive-colored hips as he thrust harder. Brindi cried out in sheer ecstasy. Her hands clutched at the chair to steady herself.

"Can't stop." He stopped deep inside of her. His large buttock muscles flexing as his orgasm shot out of him.

Brindi screamed in delight, her body convulsing, thrusting herself up and down on his hardness, and uttering words in Chinese. After long heaving moments, she opened her eyes and realized everyone was watching her. A shy smile and a deep blush stole across her face. "I'm so sorry, teacher, so sorry. I lost myself."

"That's okay. Hope some of you caught her in her state of sheer splendor." Vesper glanced at the clock on the wall. "I think it's time for a break anyway." The petite oriental girl, not used to being the center of attention, quickly donned her robe. "Don't be ashamed, Brindi, you've inspired the class. Both of you may go to the washrooms just outside to clean up and compose yourselves and quietly return."

Hans donned his robe and, with the natural grace of a Viking warrior, moved confidently down the aisle, so unlike the shaken Brindi, who nearly ran down the length of the room.

Leanne put her hand up. "Is that one of the prerequisites?"

"No," Vesper replied. "Good question. That rarely

happens. The poor girl was too far gone to be able to sit, concentrate, and draw. Actually, I call that a bonus when I've managed to put someone on the edge of their fantasies and they get off losing themselves. I hope there was something you saw in Brindi, the look in her eyes, the sweat beading on her brow that released your artistic instincts."

"Put me on the edge of my seat, and I couldn't say that Hans was in any coherent state of mind himself," one of the others added.

"True, not sure how he managed to keep himself from letting go earlier as well. Next Davis and Dennis, after Brindi returns."

Which she did in a few minutes, still looking flustered and embarrassed. "My apologies on the delay." Head down, she quietly strolled back in.

"I've nothing against my models getting that excited, after all, this is an erotic drawing workshop and that can sometimes be the outcome. If you haven't noticed I might pair you up with someone that is either the opposite of what you expect or what your fantasies may have described."

"Now guys on stage, time for a little bit of different sexuality."

They did, both disrobing, cocks already semi-hard. Dennis had some body hair, David was nearly hairless, other than what appeared to be light peach fuzz type. Neither were overly muscular and by the way they acted and talked, Leanne would have guessed both to be probably gay.

"Now, Dennis, grab a chair and sit in it. David, you're his servant and have been caught stealing. Over his knees, your penis between his legs."

He assumed the position, his hardness giving him away. Dennis closed his legs, trapping the man's erection between.

"Now, Dennis, spank him four times, hard on each cheek, and finish by resting your hand on his ass before caressing his rear."

David jumped as Dennis rained the slaps on his ass, his cock jumped as David began to fondle his hairless rear.

"Slow caresses on his reddened ass, now draw."

Leanne was amazed at the control Vesper had, but she'd probably done this several times. Would she be that dominant in the bedroom, as well?

After several minutes they stopped. "Okay, Dennis, you're obviously aroused at having to admonish a subservient male over your lap. Show us what David needs to do to relieve your frustration and show his loyalty to you."

Dennis stood up. "Get on your knees and don't move." He quickly grabbed the sash from his bathrobe and tied the man's hands behind his back. He put one hand behind David's head and drew it toward him. If they weren't a couple it was obvious Dennis was a man that was usually in control and enjoyed making others submit to him. "Now, if you're okay with it, Vesper." He turned his gaze back to the man on his knees. "Suck your master's cock or I'll have to spank you again with my leather belt this time." Dennis admonished David, taking control of the situation.

David moaned as Dennis opened his mouth and, without a condom on, shoved his uncircumcised cock down his throat.

"Slowly, very slowly, suck his cock, in and out.

Remember you must please him or he'll whip you again. Now draw." Vesper smiled, seeming to relish the idea that David had just taken over.

Pencils flew as David slowly sucked the offered cock, sometimes his tongue lathered the underside sticking out. He enjoyed being helpless and forced to suck this man's cock. Leanne knew how exciting being helpless could be, taken against your will.

After long moments, saliva adorning David's lips and Dennis' cock, Vesper called time. "Are you close?" Dennis nodded.

"You may finish yourself off in your servant's mouth, unless the servant wants a rubber first."

David licked his lips and slid the throbbing cock into his mouth. Dennis began to stroke himself as David quickened the pace of his fellating of his cock. Very quickly, Dennis groaned as he came and David held his lips over the man's throbbing cock.

Leanne had never watched another man pleasure another. She guessed it was like two women together. Each instinctively knew how to please each other. That she knew all too well.

"Good, servant boy. I'll expect that in the future if you wish to be my employee."

"I'm glad I could please my master and will do so as requested in the future." He licked the man's cock clean.

"I do think the energy is very erotic tonight, must be the nearly full moon outside. It does stir the blood and desires."

Dennis untied David and the two put their robes on, exiting the stage. Leanne wanted to ask Vesper later if they were a couple or just two men that happened to join the class admitting they either were gay or had fantasies.

"Ingrid and Tom next."

A tall, lanky Swedish lady got up quickly, she unpinned her platinum hair, putting on a show. She was lean, near model material, although about ten pounds too heavy by supermodel dimensions, which were two twigs under stick size. It was obvious to all that she had no fear of being on stage and rather relished the thought of others watching her naked. She disrobed before getting on the dais. Small breasts sat pert on her chest, her small triangle of pubic hair was as blonde as her head.

A true blonde then, Leanne thought.

Tom got up rather slowly. He tightened his robe and slowly walked to the stage adjusting his glasses as he did. Unlike Hans or the other two, Tom was thin and almost as pale as Ingrid. He looked very nervous and like he belonged in front of a computer desk calculating figures, not posing naked in front of a crowd.

Some very interesting people here, not just your artsy kinda electic type of crowd. Leanne mused. Then again she'd never really been in any kind of art classes, wasn't sure really what artsy-fartsy types should look like. Other than weird shawls thrown over their shoulders, hair in some type of bizarre do and a pencil stuck behind their ear. She guessed some wouldn't have guessed she was into drawing either. This class was beginning to make her realize it took all kinds to make the world go around and one really didn't know what passions others possessed inside.

"Ingrid, lay on your back, legs apart and folded. Tom, place your head between her legs."

He did, holding his head about a foot from the golden view of her vagina.

"No, closer. I want you to be able to smell her arousal and, if I had asked, reach out with your tongue and lick her."

He swallowed and removed his glasses before bending down again. Leanne would have guessed he'd never seen a pussy up close, for real.

"Put your hands around her hips and Ingrid place those lovely legs on his back."

As she did, they naturally unfolded, opening her up even further.

"Now, Tom, you are about to lick those gorgeous blonde curls. Can you smell her arousal?"

"Oh, yes." The crowd could see him stiffening as he inhaled her musky fragrance.

"Smells can stimulate us quite a lot sometimes. I can see they work well for Tom."

"Now draw."

Leanne couldn't believe how much of a turn-on this class was. Would she be able to control herself on stage? She was wet now. Now she knew why Vesper had the class fill out the form, some of the questions helped her to decide who to pick and what fantasies they had inside of them.

Vesper kept glancing her way and whispered as she walked by, "Nice strokes." Her hand lightly squeezed Leanne's shoulder.

Leanne imagined Tom to be near virginal, he probably had little experience with women and much more with internet porn than the real McCoy. His eyes stayed glued to the blonde lips before him. Probably memorizing every fold, every hair for later reference when he was pleasuring himself, she surmised.

Minutes later, as Tom dripped sweat Vesper approached the dais. "Okay, finish up. Now, Ingrid, you've turned this young man on. Tom, put on a rubber and get on your back. Ingrid, get on top, and if you don't want to, you don't have to insert him in you. Instead slide your pussy along his cock, like your hand would if you were performing fellatio on him."

"I think he needs a little lube first."

Ingrid spread her long thin legs over him and lowered herself down over his erect cock. Tom looked mortified as she swallowed his cock inside her and slide down the entire length without a condom on.

Either a brave or very stupid girl, Leanne thought.

"I've never, oh God," Tom gasped as she moved expertly over him.

He was bound to come in seconds, Leanne guessed.

"I think Ingrid you best pull out or we'll have an accident here, before anyone gets a chance to put pencil to paper."

She did and began to slide her wet pussy along his throbbing cock, masturbating herself along the length of his rigid penis. It was obvious she enjoyed teasing him and being in control. Ingrid smiled as she leaned over, hands on his chest, and kissed him. She continued to rub herself up and down on his cock.

"Nice and slow. Now draw."

Most of the class was watching to see how long poor Tom would last, and about two minutes later he cried out as a stream of his cum spurted up along her back.

"Sorry, so sorry," Tom apologized.

"I think you've enjoyed yourself a little too much. Can I ask without embarrassing you is this your first time?"

"With someone, yes." He closed his eyes as Ingrid kept humping herself along his cock. She was obviously excited by making him cum just by rubbing herself along him. Control, Leanne knew, can be as addictive as submission.

"Now we've another five minutes of drawing time, lay there and enjoy what she's doing to you."

After a few minutes, Vesper yelled stop and allowed Tom to go to the washrooms to clean himself up after he wiped her down with his robe.

"Let me take you to my room after class and make up for the embarrassment." Ingrid kissed him on the cheek as he slid his glasses back on and the lanky Swede got off him.

"Okay, next up Sandra and Leon, as we wait for Tom after our unfortunate accident."

Sandra was a very Goth-looking girl, dark hair, very pale complexion, with a nose and lip ring. Tattoos ranged up and down her arms, and Leanne thought probably over the rest of her as well. She had very large breasts and next to Vesper's the largest in the room.

Leon was a large black man who had been staring at her chest most of the night.

Hell, Leanne thought, so had I.

"Leon, take your robe and get behind Sandra. Pull hers down to her waist. Grab her breast with one hand and pull her face to you with the other. You're in control, she is yours. Yours alone."

Her breasts were decorated with tattoos of roses and orchids, which flowed down her belly. Nipple rings jutted from the ends of her already erect nipples.

"You are helpless in the hands of this big black stud, who wants you and will take you. Now nice and slow, Leon, roll her lovely pierced nipple between your fingers."

Her nearly snow-white skin in sharp contrast against his ebony sheen. She moaned loudly as he fondled her breast and nipple, holding her face to his. Their eyes open, the desire of both evident.

"Go ahead and kiss her. Now draw."

They kissed slowly as his hand cupped and fondled her breast. Occasionally tweaking her nipple and pulling on the ring attached to it. Sandra moaned deeply.

"Okay, stop."

Sandra panting, turned around, flung her arms around his neck, and kissed him deeply. It was obvious she wanted to straddle him right then and there.

"He excites you."

"Yes, very much so."

"On all fours, Sandra, Leon behind her. Your cock between her ass cheeks, slowly rub yourself along her crack. He's getting ready to take your ass. Does that turn you on?"

"Yes," she said. "So dirty and taken."

"Okay, now play with yourself with one hand while he rubs himself on you."

She reached between her legs with one hand and began to finger herself. Her fingers rubbed on her clit while the big black man slid his large hard cock along her ass cheeks. His arousal evident as slickness oozed from his cock.

"Draw. Knowing he wants your ass. His hunger, to

take you deep in a place no one's ever had you."

Sandra moaned constantly as she played with herself. When they were done after Vesper called time, she turned to Leon and whispered to him.

"What did you say to Leon if I can ask?" Vesper asked.

"He can take me to his room and take me there if he wanted." She blushed.

"Leon, what do you say to that?"

"Try and stop me." He grunted with his sonorous voice.

Vesper stared at Leanne as she called up two women next and licked her lip. Cheryl was a very well-built redhead, about five foot ten. Tina, a small petite blonde. They both dropped their respective robes.

Tina looked at Cheryl's very red, well-cropped bush as they got on stage.

"Well then, either of you ever been kissed sexually by another woman."

"Yes," Cheryl said. Tina nodded no, her arousal in her eyes spoke of something totally different.

"Yet, I see the thought of being in a stronger woman's arms seems to excite you, doesn't it, Tina?" Tina nodded side to side weakly.

"Cheryl, kiss her hard now, I think she's lying."

Cheryl grabbed the back of her head and pulled Tina's small mouth to hers. Their breasts crushed together. Cheryl aggressively frenched the petite blonde. Tina groaned, her nipples hardening in an instant as she surrendered to the redhead's tongue invading her mouth. Melting into her body, her arms wrapping around the taller woman.

"Thought so. Most women have some sort of

lesbian instincts." She walked up to the two women. "Keep kissing her and let me place your hands." She kept Cheryl's one hand on the back of Tina's head and the other cupping Tina's ass.

She took one of the blonde's hands and shoved it between Cheryl's legs. The other went around her back. "You are hers, Tina. All hers. Feel her wetness, she wants you, and inside you know behind the denial you want to satisfy her. When Cheryl's done kissing you, she may push you to your knees and force your mouth against her wet pussy. Does that excite you?"

The blonde groaned into Cheryl's mouth.

"Stroke her," Vesper commanded.

Tina did, and Cheryl moaned back.

"Draw."

The slow sensuality of the moment struck Leanne. She remembered being taken by Sam in her store in a similar fashion. Her first lesbian experiment and one that changed her view on sex with other women. She squirmed in her seat.

Vesper walked up to her and whispered into her ear. "Does that turn you on?" Her breath hot in her ear.

"Yes." She looked up at Vesper.

"I want you like that in my arms later."

Leanne shuddered, she had been pretty certain Vesper had lesbian tendencies, now there was no doubt. She watched the two women kissing deeply.

"Time."

"Now, Tina, on your knees and, Cheryl, hold Tina's face to your pussy. Make her eat you out."

"With my pleasure." The tall redhead moaned. "I wanted her tongue there all the time we were kissing."

She pushed the shaken blonde to her knees and

pulled her face into her pelvic area. She lifted one leg and placed it behind the blonde's back. "You aren't going anywhere, darling."

"Now go ahead and lick your first woman. Slow, nice and slow."

Everyone watched as Cheryl rubbed her auburn curls along Tina's mouth. Tina began to lap the pussy in front of her, relishing its musky juices. Cheryl slowly rubbed herself on the blonde's tongue and mouth. She arched her back thrusting her breasts forward, obviously enjoying the oral stimulation.

"Hold that pose."

After a few long moments, Vesper looked at her watch. "Time is nearly up. Cheryl, are you close?"

"Yes," she moaned as she continued to masturbate herself on the blonde's face. The sheer pleasure on her face evident.

"Now, does everyone want to watch Tina make Cheryl orgasm on her mouth?" Everyone agreed.

"Go ahead and move however you need to."

Cheryl lowered her one leg and put both of her hands behind the head of the blonde servicing her pussy with obvious delight. Cheryl began to thrust herself harder and faster, riding the blonde's face, as her orgasm began to overtake her. "Oh God," she moaned as she came, shuddering on the tongue of the blonde. Holding herself still as Tina kept licking away in relish until Cheryl cried out, "Stop."

Tina rose before the shaking redhead and kissed her lips. "So hot. That was unbelievable, I'd like to do that with you again." They kissed slowly.

Cheryl looked down at her. "I brought a strap-on along just in case." Tina's eyes opened at the thought of being fucked by another woman.

"I've one more set, those of you who'd like to retire to your rooms can leave if you like, or use the washrooms, take a break. This has been a most stimulating class. We'll be serving mulled wine, cheese, and crackers after dark on the outside patio in about half an hour. For those of you with the energy to get out of your beds and talk about your artistic experiences here or show us some of your drafts."

Cheryl grabbed Tina by the hand as they stood on the dais. "In my room you're going. I need to return the favor." She grabbed her hand and led her out the door. Everyone except Leanne and Brian, Vesper's boyfriend, rose. Soon there were only the three of them.

"Did that arouse you?"

"Oh, yes."

"Come here, Leanne," Vesper commanded. As she stepped on the dais, Vesper pulled her to her lips and kissed her deeply.

Vesper's tongue hungrily swept into Leanne's mouth.

Finally, they parted.

"Do all the classes turn out to be this erotic?"

"No, some are just so-so. This one was extremely arousing. Like I said at the beginning, that's why I ask a lot of personal questions on the form you fill out, and I try to get people matched up with each other. Now you, I've saved for Brian and myself. But me first." She untied her bathrobe and opened Leanne's. "Tie yours around me, and I'll do the same." Vesper pulled her hands out of her sleeves and wrapped them around Leanne. Leanne did the same. "Only you will know what I'm doing to you." One hand ran up and down

Leanne's back as the other began to caress her between the legs. Vesper lowered her hand until it cupped Leanne's ass and began to kiss her. All Brian could see was the two women kissing under the robes.

Vesper's large pillowy breasts crushed against hers. Leanne reached up to fondle Vesper's breasts as their legs went between each other's. Vesper began to rub herself on Leanne's thigh. "While a woman's mouth on my pussy is great. I love rubbing or masturbating with my female lovers. Ever tribbed?"

"No." The thought was a sudden turn-on. She never did it with Amanda.

"Very sensual and something only two women can do together. I want to do that with you." Leanne gasped.

"To the ground." Leanne pulled their robes apart and Leanne sank to the ground. Vesper got on top of her between her open legs and lowered her pussy to Leanne's. The slickness of each other added to the heat generated. Vesper held Leanne's one leg up as she began to rub herself back and forth. Vesper quickly bucked as her orgasm began to overtake her. The two moaned as they rubbed their pussies together. Vesper on top holding onto Leanne's knee as she began to buck hard. She fell forward kissing Leanne softly on the lips. "Sorry, I was a bit quick. I've been thinking of doing that all day with you and watching Cheryl and Tina really excited me. Perhaps you'd like something harder in you to get off."

Vesper stood up on shaky legs and behind her Brian approached, his arousal very evident as he slipped a condom on. He walked up, opened Leanne's legs, and slid himself quickly into her wetness. Leanne grunted as his hard cock filled her. "Oh fuck." The sheer sensation of him entering her all at once set her nerves on fire.

Brian slowly thrust himself into her as he sat on his knees. Vesper leaned over and kissed Leanne. "Ready to eat me?"

"Yes."

Vesper spread her legs over Leanne's face and lowered herself to Leanne's mouth. She leaned over and kissed her boyfriend as he continued to slowly fuck the strawberry blonde. Leanne licked away at the offered pussy. Vesper reached down and gently rubbed Leanne's clit. "If we time this right we might have a three-way orgasm."

The three kept their rhythm in time to each other. Soon, Leanne could feel herself building as she sucked on Vesper's enlarged clit. Lost in the deliciousness of the moment as he thrust hard into her. "Keep sucking my clit, oh," Vesper cried as she returned to kissing Brian.

Brian slowed down, trying to time himself and not come too early.

Vesper gasped. "Oh, it's starting again." She continued fingering Leanne as she thrust away on her face, her orgasm beginning to build inside. Brian, unable to control himself, began to fuck Leanne hard and fast. She cried out as he slammed himself into her. All three moaned as their orgasms overtook them.

Claps rang out from the back of the room as most had returned and were applauding the scene before them.

"Damn, didn't get a chance to get my water colors." Sandra smirked as she and Leon entered the room.

Tom looked like he'd had his socks blown into a million pieces by Ingrid, and Brindi looked much the same after most likely being stuffed by Hans's massive cock. Leanne wondered if even she could have got that porn-sized weapon into her. She hadn't, nor cared that the three of them had an audience.

Vesper sank against Brian. "Oh fuck, that was one of my best orgasms ever."

"Now there's a very erotic picture for me to remember for later," Ingrid spurted out.

"Give me a moment to compose myself," Vesper gasped. Leanne had never seen her so flustered. "Before I bring out the crackers and cheese. Wine's already brewing out by the kilns."

An hour later, everyone had gathered outside in the cool mountain air, as usual when the sun went down so did the temp. Vesper addressed the group, "Now some of you might be into each other as couples and after tonight that is okay. Many people have sent me emails saying they've gotten together due to being here at this course. I think this group is a bit more adventuresome than most, and I usually encourage everyone to be open to experimenting. So after a couple of glasses of mulled wine to loosen inhibitions, I'd like us to go back inside, and I'll spread some blankets. I've never done a group orgy, I think this crowd is up for it."

Amazingly, everyone nodded their willingness.

Once inside, Brian dimmed the lights as Vesper spread out several thick blankets. Shy Brindi flung her robe aside first and grabbed Tina's hand. "I've never desired another woman before tonight and may not again, watching you pleasure Cheryl was exciting and we are here to explore boundaries." The two kissed and fell to the ground, fondling each other and soon moved into the classic sixty-nine position.

With the wine working, its inhibition dropping fluids, David and Dennis approached Leanne. "We enjoyed watching your threesome and would like to do it with you in the center."

"Why not, I've never done it with two men." They all shed their clothes and she got on all fours. Dennis slid his hard cock into her as she began to suck David's meaty penis sheathed in its protective rubber. This she didn't expect. The others joined in all around them. Cheryl had grabbed the slim blonde and was frenching her, while expert fingers masturbated her.

Sandra was on her back having the thick Hans stuffing her with delight.

At one point, Leon had the petite Tina lifted in the air and held her up with his muscular arms as he fucked her. Virginal Tom allowed David to mount him from behind while he licked away at Sandra's offered pussy. Redheaded Cheryl even had a go at the large Norwegian. Under the moonlight streaming in, positions shifted and cries rang out through the lust-filled night until everyone lay spent.

"Wow, didn't think art could be so stimulating," Leanne muttered as she crawled into her bed very late into the night.

****

Leanne sat on her stool, the Bow Falls fell down toward her as she painted on the shore, its constant mists surging into the still mountain air. The Banff Springs Hotel behind the crowd of spruce trees, the scent of their sap sharp in the crisp air. How many had come to these shores, travelers, and honeymooners? That was the intent in the old days when the railroad ruled like the prints from her mom. To bring world-class travelers to places to stay in first-class hotels, surrounded by first-class settings. She smiled, somehow content at being alone after all that happened on this crazy road trip, it seemed fitting that she was here and at peace. Her other art classes for the last couple of weeks were more sedate and closer to what she called normal.

A cough drew her attention to the right. She spied a younger, handsome-looking man. Well at least from a distance, he looked good, perhaps if she was to get closer, he'd look more like the Hunchback of Notre Dame. Like her, he was painting and seemed to be glancing her way. If he'd been taking classes at the Banff Fine Arts school she'd have noticed him.

Curious, Leanne got up and approached him. "Excuse me, I don't mean to intrude, couldn't help but notice that you're painting, like myself. I'm Leanne Benson."

He put down his paintbrush. "Holden, James Bond Holden."

"James Bond? No relation to 007?"

"No, my parents were big fans of the movies."

He wiped paint smears off his hands before they shook. Dried paint-smudged fingertips rubbed against each other. Leanne felt the heat of his touch penetrate her in the cool of the mountain air.

"So out of curiosity, what are you painting?" *Okay, so he didn't resemble the Hunchback.* In fact, she found him fairly handsome. Dirty blond hair, impish grin, and that handsome, square-jawed face she found so masculine in men, which gave him that distinguished Bondy-type look, like he belonged more behind a tuxedo, bowtie, and the wheel of a Jaguar, than behind a paintbrush.

"You," he said bluntly.

"What?" Leanne didn't expect that, not with the mountains, the river, the falls, and everything around them that many people would cry to see and most, fall in love with.

"Well, I come here to paint the falls for the last few days and today when I got up I said to myself there's something missing from this view. Today you came, sat down and began to paint and I knew you were the missing link to my painting."

"Makes me sound rather Cro-Magnon."

"Far from it. This close you don't look remotely like a cavewoman. Care to see you as I do?" He smiled rather sincerely.

Leanne blinked, not sure what to expect when a stranger asks you to look at yourself through their eyes.

She walked around to the canvas before him. Sunlight streamed from behind her in the picture, highlighting her in silhouette against the only clothing that she appeared to be draped in, if one could call it that, sheer diaphanous silk that flowed in undulating layers over her. She sat at an easel, painting the Bow Falls falling in its own layers of misting silk behind her. Obviously naked under the garment, her breasts jutted out, dark nipples hinting at their arousal. Her long curvy legs slightly apart, one hand disappearing between them. Her head back and staring at the viewer. Her smile was slightly lusty, as if pleasuring herself to the painter of the falls.

"Oh, that's a little risqué and presumptuous of you," she blurted, yet he'd captured a sheer sensuality of herself, at peace, like she was earlier. As an artist, he was good, as a person a bit rude.

"Artistic license." He smiled very straightforward.

"Were you trying to imagine what I'd look like naked without anything on?" Or was he a Van Gogh version of a pervert? Who apparently wasn't a saint in real life either.

"As an artist, I was trying to paint an image of the serene beauty that presented itself before me as I requested to the splendor of the heavens above this morning to complete my painting."

'The splendor of the heavens above.' She never heard God or the creator, or, she blushed, herself ever called that before.

His smile deepened. "That's the artist in me, the male saw something else. An exquisite vision of strawberry blonde sexuality, sublime yet confident, highlighted in contrast against the pale of nature-caressed sunlight and backdropped on glacier-fed pristine waters."

His frankness took Leanne back. She really didn't know what to say or dare to. Nope, definitely not a Colin. Yet something about that mad quirkiness grabbed her.

"I saw a gorgeous woman and fantasized what you'd look like naked in my arms. The feel of your skin against mine as I'm in you. The taste of your lips against mine. The hunger of us being together, how you'd smell as we made love, and the sounds you'd make orgasming."

"Wow, you're forward and obviously love-starved." *And nothing like Colin, who at least had some manners and boundaries.* She should be appalled at his rude language, yet he'd said it somewhat sincerely, as a writer would reading out a story, with expression and emphasis. "I can see that your other head rules your body."

"And you're even prettier close up. Besides, you asked, as an artist, I like to engage all of my senses."

Colin, who while young, with a similar sense of humor, was more sincere, and she sensed a little more tolerant of her needs. No, James Holden, was not like any man she'd ever met. Everything he said threw her, and she'd met many people in her times as a real estate agent. Even a ghost who knew how to drag shit out of her and another who dragged a lot more out of her on this trip. Still, it was obvious he meant no real offense.

"I've been told you don't get anywhere in life by not asking for what you want."

"Okay." She wanted to play along, not knowing where this was going. "James Holden, what is it you truly want?"

"You, that is obvious." He thought for a moment. "Tonight it is a nearly full moon. I would like to picnic with you, at midnight here under the pines and the stars. Some wine and a little finger food."

Leanne blinked. This was the oddest proposition she ever had. "I'll bring a blanket, wine, glasses, and food to nibble on. You only have to bring yourself."

She glanced at her watch. "I've a massage waiting for me in a few minutes, gotta go. But, my good man," she said in a high English accent, "your proposal sounds rather inviting. You may catch me under the trees at the river's edge highlighted in the moonlight."

Leanne turned and before he could respond, she strolled back to her easel and packed it up. One backward glance as she loaded up her car caught him staring at her, his paintbrush dancing over the canvas. He may have been a mad artist, but he intrigued her. She wondered if he put as much passion into his lovemaking as he did his painting.

****

Leanne spread the blanket out under a large pine tree by the edge of the Bow River. She was a little early, and he hadn't shown yet. The three-quarter moon hung in the sky just clearing the Rockies, the falls gurgled in the background. Even in the summer, once the sun went down it chilled quickly. She tucked herself tighter in the long coat she had on. She placed the bottle of Merlot before her along with two glasses and the bottle opener. If he didn't show in five minutes, she'd crack the bottle open and begin to enjoy herself without him. Leanne was certain by the look in his eyes, he'd be coming. She just believed in being punctual, which usually meant being five minutes early, from her days of selling real estate. It never looked good to a client if she was late, especially the ones in Beverly Hills that had lots of money and typically little time.

Headlights of an approaching car flooded the area and pulled up beside hers, the only two in the parking lot. She could see it was James as he got out of his new Jaguar XJ. From her involvement with the Hollywood crowd, she knew it was worth a few bucks.

Well, she thought to herself, either he's got money or daddy's looking after him. She waved at him to catch his attention.

He approached looking very distinguished, wearing

a black suit jacket and pants, with a white shirt and bowtie. "Well, funny finding you here." He smiled as he put down the woven picnic basket, leaned over, and kissed her cheek. "I thought you seemed flattered by my middle name and decided I'd do the secret agent look to go along with my car. You know us special operatives, we always get our women."

Leanne was a bit startled by his forwardness and dress, yet that instantly told her that he had no qualms about going for what he wanted and probably had some class to himself. He placed several containers of various cheeses, crackers, and cut-up vegetables on the blanket. "I hope you didn't rent the car just for this occasion, and I thought it was the RCMP that always gets their man?"

"Car's mine, and they are not my type. RCMP can have the guys, I stick to the opposite sex. So, the pâté is one of smoked salmon and chicken with coriander and lemon. Very nice. Now, lovely lady, I do believe it is up to the gentleman to open the wine."

"Can I have your shoe?"

"My shoe?"

"Yes, need to open the wine. Didn't bring a corkscrew, however, just to prove my secret agent capabilities, watch."

She did, puzzled as he pulled off the wrap and placed the very expensive Chateau Margaux Bordeaux red inside her shoe. Was he utterly mad or some kind of kinky pervert? She knew that bottle was worth several hundred.

"Well, I do have an opener but somehow I think this is a little more intimate and awe-inspiring." He took the shoe and tapped it against the spruce tree several times. Slowly the cork backed its way out of the bottle until he could pull it free with his hand.

"Your shoe back, unscathed."

"Wow," she said as he poured the wine and gave her a glass before pouring himself one. "I didn't expect Mr. Bond himself to arrive. You definitely have a few tricks up your sleeve. Does the Jag have a hidden ejector seat if I don't behave?"

"No, the heater and built-in vibrator I'm told are rather pleasant. Why the long coat, are you that cold already?"

"Well, I was a bit too shy to walk out of the hotel dressed like this." Leanne stood up and shed the coat. The moonlight caught the layers of silk draped over her in a shimmer. Her nipples hardened in the cool air, underneath she had nothing on. She was sure he could see the outline of her pubic hair cut in a nice vee.

"Stunning, even Van Gogh, Boldini, or Picasso couldn't paint that incredible beauty." His eyes widened in true appreciation.

"Besides, Mr. Bond…er…Holden, this, as they say in the movies, is mainly for your eyes only."

She knew he could see the outline of her legs under the silk, and he tried not to stare at the slight jostle of her breasts as she sat down.

"Now, I don't have to imagine what you look like underneath the silks in my painting. Absolutely stunning."

He took out three little metal pots and with a lighter, lit up the incense cones within them. The area soon filled with aromas of patchouli, sandalwood, and lavender.

Leanne inhaled deeply. "Nice touch, I like

engaging the senses. By the way, do you always carry very expensive wine around in the trunk of your car?"

"You never know when I might need to seduce some damsel in silk." He smiled at her as he sipped his wine.

"Mr. Holden, how forward of you." She teased in a coy voice. "Do you expect to part these layers of silk and avail yourself of my wares?"

He smiled softly as he placed a little of the pâté and cheese on a cracker and offered it to her. The scents of pine and incense filtering the air in the darkness lent itself to the hush of the water's gurgle as they talked. "I reckon by the fact you are here, dressed as you are, that getting past those veils was already on the cards. I am but a true gentleman and shall keep these inquisitive hands in check. Until the lady so desires my touch."

Leanne could feel the expensive wine already loosening her inhibitions as she nibbled delicately at the offered cracker from his hand. He moved closer until he sat beside her. The warmth of his body added to the heat between them. "I do think you may presume correct. This woman is flattered by your proposal and indeed honored to be painted by you." She reached up and as she tasted the rest of the cracker, she licked at his finger. "I always make sure I reward my admirers."

"Do you now?" He watched her lips wrap around his finger as she sucked it gently into her mouth. James moaned in delight.

"Well, I'm glad you like to show your admiration. Tell me about yourself," he asked as he gulped down his wine.

"Well, I work in Beverly Hills, an exclusive real estate agent. Sell to the stars."

"Met any really big names?"

Leanne named a few. What she didn't say is that most of those she'd seen naked and usually had sex with. She didn't really think this would go much further than tonight. While he wasn't a Colin, more mature and truly off the wall. But as the romance books said, if he didn't grab her and make her shake inside, then he wasn't the one. Handsome, romantic, sure. Or was it just her holding back? Afraid to get involved long-term yet? Leanne already knew her answer.

"Why are you here?"

"Just last month, I lost my dad and my husband on the same day. Virtually at the same time. I'd always wanted to spend time painting and after the dust settled I had lots of money and no one to spend it with. I had someone to run the business and decided to get away on a road trip. So here I am."

"Trying to get on with your life?"

"Yes." She sipped at her wine and continued nibbling away at the food he'd brought.

As they talked, she leaned into him. James put his arm around her and kissed her head. The man was very considerate and sensitive. She leaned back against his chest, enjoying the closeness of the moment. He grabbed bits of cheese to bring to her lips. Leanne accepted and nibbled at his fingers again. "You?"

"I'm actually here on a conference, staying at the Banff Springs. Similar story, my dad died a few years ago. I was well off already, used the money to start an internet company. Well, it took off, I sold the rights to an online company for a tidy sum, and still take some nice royalties. During all of this preoccupation with work, my wife left me for my pool boy. So I decided to hang out these last three years. Like you, always wanted to paint, take a few courses, and see what I want to try my hand at for my next business move."

"Get lonely? I think that's the hardest part at first. Sleeping by myself."

"Yeah, at first. True. I quite enjoy it now. No one to tie me down, nor was I ever one to try bondage. Don't have to work, can draw, and paint all I want. Of course, a little side highlight of fun and romance is a nice distraction." He pulled her face toward him and kissed her softly. The hunger and want evident on his lips. He caressed her face.

She looked into his eyes.

"You, I find rather stunning. Always wanted to go out with a redhead. Are you as fiery as your reputation?"

"Well, if fire transposes to passion then lay back and let me show you."

"Oh, I do like a lady in charge." James smiled as Leanne turned around and pushed him back to the blanket.

"Well, Mr. Bond." She sat over him as he lay on the ground. She felt his hardness thrusting against his trousers as she leaned over and kissed his waiting lips.

His hands parted the folds of silk until they found her breasts, nipples already hard from the cool air and her own arousal. Wetness seeped from her. "Just lay back and watch what a woman in charge can do to you."

She rubbed herself on his protruding tent as his hands gently worshipped her body.

"Have you a rubber?"

"Of course, an agent always comes prepared—in

my right vest pocket."

She reached in and pulled it out. "Now, Mr. Bond, do keep yourself busy while I put this on, and I hope you mean it when you say an agent always comes." Leanne stood up and turned around. She lowered her pussy over his face. James began to lap away at her wet slit as she leaned down and pulled his zipper down with her teeth. She rubbed herself on his mouth, relishing his rough tongue on her. His hard, circumcised cock sprung free, its head red and engorged.

Leanne licked her lips and once moistened, slid her mouth down the entire length.

"Oh, fuck. That is incredible," he moaned into her pussy.

She pulled herself back with her lips wrapped tightly around him in a sucking motion. Opening her mouth, she slid down his throbbing cock again.

James moaned, his hands cupping her rear. She continued to fellate him for a couple of minutes. Loving the fact his cock wasn't too large and wasn't gagging her as it filled her mouth. "I don't think it will take much to finish you off."

"I agree," he moaned as his mouth slid the length of her wet pussy lips. He was good, nothing, however, compared to some of the women that she'd been with.

Leanne released his cock and grabbed for the rubber. She wrapped it around his throbbing penis. Turning, Leanne grunted as she sat down on him, his hardness filling her. She spread the silk around them, so no one could see what they were doing. Only an owl nearby seemed to hoot its shock to the moon and stars. Right now, she didn't care as she slid her G-spot against the hard knob throbbing inside of her. "Now,

Mr. Bond, time to talk as I torture you with my pussy." Leanne slowly bucked against the cock buried inside of her.

"Six, forty-two, eighteen, seventy-two, nine, and twelve. The winning lottery numbers to this week's draw and my debit pin number is one-six-four-one-two. I'll tell you anything right about now. God, you're good."

"That's the plan, total surrender, my dear agent."

"I'm yours. Man, do I like this kind of torture. You evil temptress, you take great pleasure in making me suffer in erotic agony."

She tightened her vaginal muscles and squeezed herself around him as she lifted and released as she slid down his cock. "I can say I enjoy dishing out the torture myself. Oh, very delicious."

"You wicked, seductive woman. I thought it was me that was supposed to be seducing you and not the other way around."

Leanne kept stroking him. She rather enjoyed being on top for once, working him with her muscles, being in control. All, too quickly she could feel herself building. He pulled on the back of her head, brought their lips together, and began to thrust hard upward as they kissed. They groaned together as Leanne felt the hot wash of sperm erupting into the condom.

She grabbed his hands and pinned them beside his body. "My turn." Leanne began to hump herself on his hard cock. Knowing he'd subside soon and wanting to get herself off first. She bucked fast, rubbing his knob against her. The tremors from within quickly cascaded through her as she threw her head back.

Leanne collapsed into his arms. They lay together

for several moments, kissing.

"Well, safe to say my mission has been compromised."

"That it has, Mr. Bond. Got any more wine and cheese left before we proceed to round number two?"

"Two? Lady, after the first one, I'll go get an entire case of the stuff if needed. That was amazing."

"Sure was, didn't think I could get you eating out of my hand."

"Or eating other bits for that matter." They laughed together as a wolf howled into the dark and somewhere the owl responded before it flew off.

She liked him, but enough to want to be with him for the rest of her life? Unlikely, that man should knock her off her socks, take her breath away at the first touch, look, or kiss. Or so the romance novels would lead her to believe. Vesper and Brian seemed more her style, and being part of a threesome seemed even more exciting, thinking about all the possibilities. James was different, almost eccentric, a self-made man, which in itself was a turn-on. But the money didn't matter, because she had more than enough to last her a lifetime. More than likely his and that off-the-wall behavior would get on her nerves. Not to mention that there was something about him that led her to believe, that if married, this flirt wouldn't let a ring stop him, given the chance. Still, he was exciting, not your typical male. Maybe being an artist would make him different, flaky. At least Colin was kind attentive and affectionate. *What did that make me then*?

"Okay, round two, and let's see if we can make you talk villainess." He grabbed her by the hand and stood up, pulling her with him. He shoved Leanne up against the tree. The layers of silk did little to stop the raw bark from digging into her back. James grabbed her two arms and thrust them over her head. He held her with one hand while with the other he pulled free a condom and, after opening it with his teeth, he shoved it over the end of his again throbbing manhood.

"Oh callous do-gooder. I'll never talk." She was surprised by the strength of his grip. Leanne couldn't break free, something exciting about being taken against her will by a man who wanted her.

"Oh, you will, after my talking stick enters your vile center." He thrust himself into her in one shove. Leanne moaned in submission as he rammed the length of his hard cock into her. "Now let's see how you fare after I have my way with you." James began to thrust hard into her.

Leanne moaned again, never being taken against her will. He began to fuck her mercilessly and the more he did the more excited she became. Leanne wrapped both legs around his midsection as James pinned her to the tree. "God, you're so wet and delicious."

"Fuck me harder," she begged as he kept plunging into her.

A helpless rag doll, pinned against the bark as he hammered into her, God, she'd never been fucked with such fury and submission. Finally he hammered deep into her as he came in one hard thrust.

Leanne lay pinned against him as they kissed. His mouth possessing hers, as his cock just did.

"East thirty-two, seventy-one." She gasped, kissing his neck, biting him in tender nibbles.

"What?"

"The secret location. All my secrets are yours."

She panted, not coming. Lost in the sensations of being helpless in this male's lusts and taking all of him. Everything this virile male could thrust at and into her.

James lowered her to the ground and their blankets as they kissed into the night. His hardness slowly ebbing from inside her as the night marched on and they fell asleep victim to their exertions.

Chapter Six

After the art classes had ended, Leanne wasn't in the mood to head back to California. Janice was managing the business well and enjoying it, so she decided to check into the Fairmount Chateau at Lake Louise for a couple of weeks. It was the hotel the painting of the two women staring out the window was created from the old Canadian Pacific poster. While extremely pricey, she didn't care. Money wasn't the issue for Leanne anymore, she had more than she knew what to do with, now. She only wanted to try and repaint the same view and atmosphere as the original. That and try to discover what her mom had fallen in love with out here, besides the incredible untamed nature of the Rocky Mountains.

While the rest of the art classes weren't as erotic as Vesper's, they did help to hone her talent. She did learn that Vesper and her partner Brian were at loose ends for a week before heading back and she invited them to stay with her for the first week. Mainly to get inspiration to draw the same picture, she lied to herself.

Actually, the idea of spending a week together with Vesper and Brian after the night in the erotic art class sent a thrill through Leanne. She rather liked being part of a threesome, especially after the night with Colin and Amanda. He'd sent her a few text messages and kept saying thank you for the night with Amanda.

Apparently, the two were going out on a steady basis and they even managed to find an older lady, Anita, who was into dominating younger women and occasionally men. Match-making wasn't on her agenda on this trip, but then she really didn't know what she would discover other than her suppressed desires to express herself in her painting.

****

"So," Vesper said, "here's something we've done before to break the ice and get some painting done at the same time."

They spread out some old blankets everywhere underneath so that the carpets wouldn't be ruined. "Now Brian is going to turn the heat up a little, and you, my dear, are going to get naked in the center of the blankets."

Leanne looked at her a little puzzled before getting it. "When you said we were to do some painting this afternoon, I didn't think I would be the canvas." Leanne smiled, standing demurely before the couple one hand on her hip after she stripped.

Vesper stared at her. "The human body gives that 3D effect, especially with such nice mounds as yours."

"And rather erotic as well." Brain winked as he walked up to her and looked at Mt. Fairview out of the window and at the far end of the lake, Mt. Victoria. They had Enya playing in the background as the two walked around Leanne, appraising her naked canvas they were about to paint.

Vesper slowly ran the soft bristles of a wider brush along the bottom of Leanne's breast and along her stomach. She quivered. "I do believe our painting background is rather sensitive today."

180

Vesper ran the brush up along the inside of her thighs. She watched the hairs on Leanne's legs rise. "Very sensitive. I think she likes being stroked."

"I know she does. Let's see how much, shall we?" Each dabbled into their palettes and began to apply various colors to Leanne's body. Vesper in front and Brian in back. They painted the mountains before them in the space of that suite onto Leanne's body. Soon she was transformed into a splendor of mountains, trees, and deep blue lake. Brain painted on her back the view from the western end of the lake, looking toward the hotel. Vesper painted the opposite end, looking toward Mt. Victoria. Leanne watched in the mirror as they stroked her body with their brushes in earnest, occasionally turning around to appraise their work. Both were very good artists and despite the heavy curve of her breasts, Vesper had managed to capture the view of the mountains before them quite well. "I think you've done this before."

"Yes, usually though most of our canvasses aren't as curvy as you. Much easier to paint someone with only a thirty-two inch chest as opposed to these wonderful 36D cups."

"Ah, but there's nothing like the deep valleys between such luscious peaks." Brian laughed.

Sunlight streamed in, filling the room with a warm glow. A couple of hours later, they were done. Vesper leaned in to kiss Leanne. "I'll bet that was exciting." She wiped some paint from her cheek with a cloth.

"Like being stroked with a feather." Leanne could feel the paint drying on her, cracking as she moved slightly.

"Now, don't smudge the canvas before I get to take

a few pictures." Brian grabbed his digital camera and began to snap away, having Leanne take a few poses, so he could get shots of both sides of her.

"Now, you may smudge the artwork, my dear," Brian said as he began to take off his clothes. Vesper disrobed quickly, she hadn't anything under her robe. She wrapped her arms around Leanne and gave her a deep French kiss. Her body smeared the paints all over her while Brian clicked away a few more times. He positioned the camera and set the delay on, before quickly stripping himself and joining the two women. The camera continued to click away as the three began to touch and stroke each other. Their bodies blending into a mash of smeared pastels. Mountains, green forest, and emerald waters all smearing into a mash of abstract images. *From Leonardo to Van Gogh to Picasso.* Leanne mused and as the camera slowly kept taking pictures, she dropped to her knees.

Brian slipped on a condom, which is easier said than done when his fingers were dripping in rainbow colors, and slipped his hard cock into her from behind. Vesper lay before Leanne and pulled her face into her thick black patch. Leanne began to lick the wet slit before her as Brian slowly fucked her doggy-style. "Oh, I do love an artist that really gets into their work," Vesper gasped, holding Leanne's head to her pussy as the redhead licked and sucked away at her in earnest.

Brian picked up his pace, and Leanne could feel the thick cock hardening, knowing he would come soon. "And avidly pursues her studies." He grunted, thrusting forward hard as his orgasm shot out of him in a hurry.

Leanne moaned into Vesper's wetness as she felt

him slamming into her and Vesper kept her head pinned to her slit. The brunette thrust against her face as she began to come on her mouth. Brian pulled himself out and, leaning over, thrust his tongue along Leanne's pussy lips before sucking on her clit. Electricity fired, lancing across her as she came, too fast and too hard.

The three collapsed to the smeared blankets. "Well I think that was a great session of painting." Colors, smeared their faces and bodies as they lay heaving in exhaustion. "Yup, time to wash up and perhaps go for some lunch," Vesper uttered.

Brian looked at her and at Leanne. "Oh, I'm not sure. I think after cleaning up our equipment, I may be in the mood for another go." Vesper grasped his softening cock. "Well, I think we need to wipe the paint-stick clean and see if it would like a replay?"

****

The next morning, they decided to enact the scene on Leanne's canvas with the two women in the CP print.

They'd gone into a costume store and managed to get some riding pants, helmets, and even a short riding whip. Brian stared at Vesper, who looked right at home tapping the riding crop along her thigh. He took several pictures from different angles of the two staring out the window. He watched Vesper rub the edge of the whip on her leg as she stared at Leanne sitting on the windowsill.

Vesper walked over slowly to Leanne and put her arm around the redhead, cupping her rear. Brian clicked away. "Now, my dear, I believe this whip has given me a nice idea for a photo shoot of another nature. I also do believe you like a little domination." She slapped

Leanne's ass.

"Oh, I guess you did read my notes from your class."

"With relish. I think I'm in the mood for a little domination, and I think our friend needs to serve me."

Leanne gasped. A shudder ran through her, as memories of the night with Sam and Nancy stirred. Would Vesper be as good as Sam as a dominant?

Brian smiled as he got up. "I'm off for a hike. Do leave a little for me when I come back." He kissed Vesper on the lips and sauntered over to Leanne, kissing her on the lips as well. "I've seen her in action," he whispered in her ear. "I'm jealous, she's very good." A minute or two later, he'd washed up and grabbed his backpack on the way out.

Vesper walked up to her. "Ever been spanked or pussy-whipped?"

A deep shudder ran through the strawberry blonde. Vesper ran the whip along the edge of her lips. "Yes," she moaned softly as she inhaled. There was something erotic about the smell of leather and the effect it had being smacked against one's flesh.

"Stand up," Vesper commanded. Leanne did. "Hands by your side and don't move until I tell you." She walked behind the quaking redhead, not knowing what to expect. With one hand, Vesper flicked open the top button of her dress, with the other she lightly flicked the edge of the whip on her skin. Leanne jumped slightly. "I said don't move." She continued unbuttoning all of the buttons, each time tapping the edge of the whip to the newly exposed flesh. Leanne cried out each time before her dress fell to her knees.

Vesper placed the whip at the bottom of her thighs

and ran it up between flesh and cotton. She reached in and with her mouth unclasped Leanne's bra. Vesper ran the whip along the edge of the bra around to the swell of her breasts, and with the whip pulled Leanne's bra away. "Hands behind your back, together."

Leanne cupped her hands together behind her, knowing it would thrust her breasts forward. Vesper reached around and cupped Leanne's breasts, squeezing each nipple hard. They hardened in response. "I think you're enjoying this."

"Yes, I am, Mistress."

"Good, so am I." Vesper picked up the bra and quickly wrapped it around Leanne's hands, tying her arms together with it. She was now Vesper's to use as she liked. Leanne shook inside—this woman had done this before, probably many times.

"Yes, you may be thinking, I've some experience at this. I used to place ads in the papers and made a lot of money, as a lesbian dominatrix, who specialized in dealing with women and wives who thought they were straight. I can't remember how many wives returned later without their husbands to pay me handsomely to subjugate them, again and again. I think if your husband brought you to me, you'd be returning for more, wouldn't you?"

"Yes," was all she could mutter, already very wet.

Vesper ran the edge of her riding whip along Leanne's thigh in a light caress. A simple flick sent a throb through her. Again, along the backs of her legs, like a caress. A snap and the whip kissed her, again and again, higher each time until she caressed the roundness of Leanne's buttocks. The leather kissed her time and again, softly, but enough to let her feel the sting of its touch. Vesper leaned into her and ran her wet tongue along the subtle redness left by the whip's kiss. Leanne moaned. It was so exciting to be put into submission at the hands of a master, or in this case, mistress.

She ran the edge of the whip up into the vee between Leanne's legs and rubbed it into the gap between her pussy lips. Vesper lifted the whip to her lips. "Obviously this is exciting you. My wet kitten. Care to taste?" She brought the moist whip to Leanne's lips and she licked herself. "I intend to make you very wet, docile, and very aroused when I'm done with you."

"Yes, Mistress." Leanne was already very aroused and only wanted to release the hunger building inside. Only, she knew, and that was part of the beauty of submission, that would be a long time in coming, if her mistress so chose.

Vesper pulled on Leanne's bound wrists. She reached around and fondled Leanne's breasts which were now thrust forward, nipples hard. "My, very attractive pose." She pinched both nipples, making them even harder. Leaning in, Vesper sucked on one first, then nibbled at it with her teeth before moving to the other.

Leanne winced under the sharp sting of her teeth, which were making her nipples even more sensitive. The throb between her legs was taking over—she only wanted the cravings to stop. It would be a long night before that happened.

"My, such sensitive breasts. I do believe you like having them sucked and bitten." Vesper reached between her legs.

Leanne gasped.

"Yes, you do. I think I'm going to enjoy having

you as my plaything tonight. Now, show me how much you want to orgasm and how much you want to pleasure your mistress first." She pulled a handful of Leanne's hair back and lifted her head to Vesper's crotch. Leanne eagerly kissed the moistening panties. While Sam was good at bondage, Vesper was obviously a professional. She wanted to surrender to her true mistress, Vesper's hot pussy.

"Ah, very good and very obedient. At least you understand who your true mistress is and are eager to satisfy her." Vesper let go of her hair. She pulled Leanne to her feet and flung the naked woman over her knees. Vesper fondled her ass cheeks. "I like strawberry blondes. Your pale complexion looks very sexy in red." She swiftly slapped each cheek in light succession before increasing the severity of her blows. Leanne moaned, crying out as Vesper continued spanking her naked ass. She stopped. "Very sexy indeed." Dipping her finger between Leanne's lips. "Nice, hot, and wet, just the way I like my women. Wanting." She reached over, picked up the whip, and flicked it across her derriere and along her upper thighs. Searing heat spread even deeper into Leanne's need to orgasm. Vesper pushed her to the floor in front of her. "On your knees, legs spread wide."

Leanne did as asked, her arms tightly bound behind her. Vesper swished the whip along her breasts, red welts erupted in the whip's wake. Her nipples were on fire. Vesper leaned back in the chair and opened her legs again. "Again, show me who's your mistress."

"You are. My mistress. And your pussy." Leanne moved forward and began to kiss the moist panties with greater hunger. Her lips sought the tender flesh underneath.

"I think my docile one really wants to pleasure me."

"Yes, very much mistress."

"I can tell by the hunger in your lips." Vesper stood up and pulled off her panties. She walked over to the padded chair and sat down. Vesper slowly spread her legs open and tapped the whip just above her pussy mound. "Now, crawl on your knees and service me, and don't even dare think of coming before I do. Understand?"

The kneeling Leanne crawled forward on her hands and knees until her face was just before Vesper's wet pussy. Vesper grabbed a handful of hair, pushing her face to the wet awaiting lips.

She began to flick the whip softly against Leanne's back and rear as Leanne bent to the task of satisfying her mistress.

"Play with yourself. I want to know how much you enjoy licking your mistress' cunt." Vesper reached over and undid Leanne's hands tied in her bra. Then she grabbed the back of the woman's face and held it as she ground her pussy into it. Both women lost in their own pleasures as moans echoed through the room.

The hunger taking Leanne over, she bent to the task of licking and sucking Vesper's pussy that was mashed to her face. Sucking on her clit, she felt Vesper begin bucking. "Oh naughty girl, how did you know I like being sucked into an orgasm?" Vesper thrust her hips to Leanne's face as she spasmed in a powerful orgasm. The whip snapped along her ass a few times as Vesper came. Leanne began to convulse as well, unable to hold herself back. She cried out into Vesper's wetness as her own fingers brought her to a climax. As Vesper's shudders diminished, she stood up and stared at

Leanne on her knees. "Now my dear, kiss your true mistress."

Leanne ran her wet lips along Vesper's left thigh and across her dark hairy mound to the other thigh before leaning in and planting a soft kiss on Vesper's wet slit. "Kiss me again, with desire."

Leanne did and this time she slid her tongue deep inside Vesper's opening, as if she was frenching her.

"Now that is how a submissive kisses her mistress." Vesper bent over and kissed Leanne hard on the lips. "I think we've another hour before Brian arrives back. So lots of time for my submissive to kiss and lick me to another splendid orgasm, only slower this time. What do you think?"

"Yes, as my mistress desires." She licked her lips, knowing that more than anything in the world, she wanted to suck on Vesper's pussy some more.

It's such a thrill being made to eat another woman's pussy. Leanne smiled to herself. *Perhaps Sam was right, a Rangeress and not a Ranger is more my style.*

Epilogue

Vesper and Brian walked ahead on the trail around Lake Louise to the Teahouse. "Go ahead," Leanne yelled. "I'll catch up later." She slowed down wanting time to herself and stopped about halfway around the lake.

Alone, she stared out at the emerald waters, the sheer face of Mt. Fairview before her, its flanks running straight into the water. She inhaled deeply, the soothing mountain air, still with the smells of pine and juniper. The earth content and at rest. An indiscreet noise filtered to her ears. Leanne strained to listen as written words came to her and a single breeze stirred the air, brushing her cheek.

Tears streamed down as a soft, barely audible hum floated all around her. "This is what Mom heard." She ran back up to the couple and hugged them.

"What was back there?" Brian asked.

"Heaven. A bit of heaven." She smiled.

A word about the author...

Born on the wild Canadian prairies but tired of the winter months in Edmonton, Frank immigrated to the more temperate cedar forests of coastal British Columbia. Yes, they get snow in Chilliwack during the winter months, and on that odd occasion Frank is forced to search out the snow shovel, dust off the cobwebs and have a go. At the snow, not the cobwebs.

His run-of-the-mill day job of auto technician/service advisor seems at odds with being an inspired, off-the-wall, author, but his zest for life, the environment, and the little muses that won't let his pencil stay still, spring from his mother's Hungarian ancestry. It's the Gypsy blood, he says, which pounds through his veins with wild abandon, driving him to the realms of fantasy.

This is the muse inside, the essence of Frank Talaber.

People who have read Frank's books describe him as a natural storyteller who writes like his soul is on fire and his pencil is his voice. They go further to say that they find his books grabbingly intense and hilarious at times, screaming everyday life from such a realistic viewpoint you're drawn into his world, hook, line and plum bob, unable to stop; almost cursing that they can't set the book down, page after page. Frank takes great pride in the realism of his work, painstakingly visiting most of the locations, (obviously, only the "real-life" ones!) and he is so thorough that many readers have remarked that they can hear, taste, visualize, smell and feel the essence of the place. "It really is like being there" one remarked. There isn't a greater compliment to be made.

His tagline is Canada's Foremost Off-beat Author (also the name of his YouTube channel; check it out for his witty and informative videos) who writes in urban fantasy, science fiction, crime, spiritual, romance, erotica and comedy genres. Well, anything that comes to him, basically! Except westerns. Although he does like to ride Gangnam style; does that count?

Literature written almost beyond genres, whose compelling thoughts are freed from the depths of the heart and subconscious before being poured onto the page. Or, as he often says, "you don't have to be mad to be a writer, but it sure helps".

https://franktalaberpublishedauthor.wordpress.com/